# A NIGHT
## AT THE
# DRESLEN

STEPHANIE MCBAIN

Stephanie McBain
mcbainstephanie@gmail.com

Printed in the United States of America
First Printing 2020
First Edition 2020

ISBN 978-1-7361680-1-1

10 9 8 7 6 5 4 3 2 1

A Night at the Dreslen is a work of fiction. Names, characters, places and incidents are the products of the author's imagination or are used fictitiously. Any resemblance to actual events, locales, or persons, living or dead, is entirely coincidental.

Any passages used from The Wonderful Wizard of Oz by L. Frank Baum with pictures by W.W. Denslow, published by Hutchinson & Company, London 1924

[snebgen azentertainmentlaw.com] are in the public domain.

Cover by KO Creative

*To all the souls who dance to the beat to their own drum.*

*It's not always the easiest journey but it's so worth it.*

*Keep dancing.*

# Table of Contents

# SUMMER

# A Fresh Start

The cardboard moving boxes were each neatly labeled with their contents: Oliver's Clothes, Hannah's Belongings, Kitchen Utensils, The Good China – fragile, and like a puzzle they were perfectly placed to make optimum use of the space of the evergreen-colored minivan. Even so, the boxes were stacked to the roof making it hard but not impossible for Jack to see out of the car windows, through the rearview mirror, and concentrate on the winding interstate ahead.

Jack was an alpha male. He was tall, athletic, and despite being in his early fifties had held on to his full head of hair: dark brown with wisps of grays that outlined his ears. When he smiled, his sky blue eyes shone, and a single dimple appeared on his right cheek. It was no secret that he was a naturally handsome man whom time had been nothing but kind to. He worked long hours, early mornings and sometimes into the night, but it was a good job, one that supported his family and allowed them to live a more than comfortable lifestyle. This job was also the reason why they were moving away from the mountains of Boulder, Colorado to the pastures of Northern Oklahoma.

Oliver was Jack's eldest child and his only son. Except for the fact that they shared the adorable dimple on the right side of their cheek, they could not have been more different from one another. Oliver was slender and average height, five foot nine on a good day. His eyes were a deep chocolate, his hair a chestnut brown, with loose waves that landed slightly above his shoulders. His eyesight was poor so he wore thick-framed glasses to help him see clearly. He was most comfortable in jeans and a basic T-shirt, a tad shy and more of a sensitive soul than his father cared to acknowledge.

Oliver sat in the passenger seat gazing out the window as the landscape changed from state to state. The road trip was uneventful. There was no conversation between Jack and Oliver for neither one had anything to say. But then the radio would lose its signal and Jack would scan the channels until he found a station he thought they both wouldn't hate. "What about this one?" Jack would ask.

"Fine," Oliver replied.

And that was it, until they drove out of signal again and then repeated the same exact exchange of words or lack thereof.

~ ~ ~

After a few long days of driving they had arrived at their destination. Jack pulled up to an enormous, tan brick home with a wraparound driveway, freshly cut grass, and beautiful landscape on a nice plot of land. "We're here," he said as he turned off the ignition. He stared up at the home. "Isn't she a beauty?" He then turned to Oliver and forced a smile. "You know, Oliver, I think you're going to like it here. It's a fresh start. A chance to fit in."

Oliver stared up at the house.

"Promise me you'll give it a shot?"

Oliver nodded yes, though when he spoke his tone was less than enthusiastic. "Sure, Dad."

"Atta boy." Jack smiled as he gave two solid pats to Oliver's shoulder and exited the van.

A burgundy car pulled up behind them and out stepped Grace. Grace was a beautiful woman. She was an excellent wife and an even more impeccable mother. She was the kind of person who believed in the power of prayer, chose to love unconditionally, and her soft demeanor was powerful enough that even an alpha male like Jack fell to her graces. She walked over to Jack and put her arm around him. "It's beautiful, honey, just like the pictures," she said as she tucked her long, champagne-colored hair behind her ear and admired their new home.

"I knew you'd like it. Wait till you see the inside."

They snuck in a simple kiss before Hannah hopped out of the car.

"Woah," Hannah gasped. "This is our house? It looks just like a castle."

She wasn't wrong, this house was three times the square footage than the one they left in Boulder and to a six-year-old the circular driveway was straight out of a fairy tale. To Hannah, it resembled a castle that belonged to a princess. To Jack it was a career milestone. To Grace, as long as her family was together, she was confident she could make any house a home. And to Oliver it was just another house in another town that he wouldn't fit into and honestly didn't care to.

"Okay everyone, grab a box, let's head inside," Jack said.

Hannah jumped with excitement. "This is so cool! I get my own room, right?"

"Of course you do, princess."

"Just making sure. Mom, what's for dinner? I'm sooo hungry."

"Once we get the boxes in, I'll make you a snack, but we must unpack first."

They all grabbed a box. "Last one in is a rotten egg!" Hannah exclaimed. Her innocence was pure, like most six-year-olds'. Jack and Grace followed Hannah inside. Oliver was the rotten egg.

~ ~ ~

The day quickly turned to night, and their move had been completed. Jack worked in finance and was very successful at it. His family had moved three times so far, supporting him as he worked his way up the chain of the company. This last promotion made every late night, every work trip, and every time he moved his family to a new state, a new city, a new home worth it. Grace remembered when Jack first told her about the move. He had surprised her with a beautiful date night at a fancy steakhouse. It was a romantic evening and then the dessert came. That was when he told her about the move and with his motive out in the open suddenly the dinner lost a bit of its meaning. She didn't want to relocate anymore, she thought it would be better for the family if they were able to set down roots for once, but she knew that this move was important to Jack. It was an opportunity he'd worked very hard for. Grace agreed to the move on one condition; that this would be their last, at least till Hannah was grown. Jack agreed, so they made their arrangements, packed up their things and here they were.

Grace stood in the kitchen. "Okay, we are all done," she said as she placed the last of the dishes in the cupboard and proceeded to break down the boxes. Jack's company had moving down to a science. She thought to herself how grateful she was that once again the company had done all the heavy lifting weeks ago and all she had to move in was the small stuff and some personal items. Jack walked up behind her and wrapped his arms around her waist. He gently began kissing her neck.

"I hope we did the right thing moving here," she said.

"The economy's in the dump, Grace. I'm in a good position with this company and they've been very generous to us."

"I know, I know, I just worry about the kids adjusting again."

"Don't waste a worry. Moving builds character. Besides, look at her." Jack pointed to Hannah who lay spread out on the beige area rug that covered the cherry oak wood floor in the living room. She held a teal-blue crayon and scribbled over the cow in her farm animal coloring book as she watched the latest child program phenomenon. "See, she's adjusting just fine," he observed. "How did we get so lucky?"

Grace smiled. He sneaked another kiss, but Grace pulled back this time. "She's not the one I'm worried about."

And like clockwork a faint roar of a vacuum came from Oliver's room. The howl traveled down the stairs and echoed into the kitchen, landing like an irritating sound of a continuous hum on the tips of their eardrums. Grace and Jack looked upwards. They knew what was happening. Oliver was at it again. They let out a sigh as both of their hearts gradually sank. Grace placed her hand on Jack's cheek and held him close. "I'll go," she said as she turned and disappeared up the stairs.

~  ~  ~

Oliver's room was dark, lit only by a tiny black lamp that stood in the corner of the room. His walls were an olive green and his bedroom set was a deep gray with matching night stands on each side of the bed and a similarly shaded curtain lined his windows. His sheets were as black as the night sky and neatly displayed on the walls were wooden shelves that contained a couple framed pieces of artwork and a single family photo. Close to the door sat a gray wooden desk where charcoal sketches on drawing paper lay about. On the other side of the room by the closet there were framed images of U2, John Mayer, Pink Floyd, and Bruce Springsteen; in his opinion, with which many would agree, some of the best musical and lyrical artists of all time. Oliver had no desire to play an instrument, but he felt connected to their music. He was aware of the deeper meaning in their art and could appreciate it. The songs they sang, the lyrics they wrote, and the stories they told were not always the most pleasant of themes, but each contained an underlining truth that spoke to his soul. When he was bored or inspired, he would play them in the background as he drew stunning works of art. Many times, he would become intrigued by one song in particular and play it over and over again in one continuous flow. It was no secret that the chosen song often mirrored his current state of mind. For the past few weeks his song of choice has been "Comfortable Numb" by Pink Floyd. And that's exactly how Oliver experienced his life. Lonely, misunderstood, and breathing but when it came to living in the world outside of his walls, he was numb.

Grace knew that when she heard that music coming from the halls she would peek in and see her sweet boy sitting at his desk, focused and diving deep into the dark, sadness of his core and expelling haunting emotions in the form of the most beautiful pieces of hand-drawn art. It was talent that she didn't understand the origins of but deeply admired. She was impressed by her son's natural talent. It was truly a gift. His art work was devastatingly gorgeous.

But tonight, there was no music playing, just the horrible and familiar sound of that vacuum. The roar of the vacuum was a sound Grace was all too familiar with but for unpleasant reasons. When Jack and Grace Roads heard the vacuum coming from Oliver's room, they knew that he was not in a calm head space. From their understanding it was a type of coping mechanism where he was attempting to grab ahold of something, anything he could to feel slightly in control.

Since Oliver was a young boy, he had been particular. He was overly analytical, anxious and cautious about everything but perhaps his most easily recognizable trait was his tidiness. Every item had a place; every picture on the wall needed to be straight, every loose paper picked up, and every speck on the rug sucked into the vacuum till it was spotless. Kids in school called him a neat freak, but his doctors called it a mild case of obsessive compulsive disorder, OCD. From an outsider looking in, the OCD combined with his anxiousness seemed like a very difficult way to live. Grace felt hopeless as a mother. Nothing she did could change his constant feelings of worry, nervousness, and unease. On the outside Grace accepted it and gave her love openly, but inside she secretly hoped that he would eventually outgrow this, but that didn't happen. This past February, when Oliver turned nineteen, she decided to do what every good mother does. Love her son for exactly who he was, even if her inability to understand him was hurting her heart. Is he happy? she wondered. This was a constant concern of hers.

She walked up the stairs and made her way across the hallway. She saw a beam of light coming from his open door. She took a deep breath into her lungs and out again to calm her emotions. She then proceeded into the room. She leaned comfortably on the side of the door frame, watching Oliver with intense focus push and pull the vacuum back and forth over the already tidy and, most would say, perfect rug.

"Oliver, Oliver!" she said from the door frame.

He couldn't hear her voice over the rumble of the vacuum.

She shouted louder, "Oliver!" Suddenly he turned around. He looked at her as sweat glistened on his forehead.

He turned off the vacuum. He eyes wandered as he waited for her to speak.

"You okay?" she asked.

"Yeah. Just vacuuming this rug. It got dusty in the move."

"Oh."

"Probably wasn't wrapped properly."

Grace nodded. "Are you nervous about the new city?"

He shrugged his shoulders. It was a rhetorical question; the vacuum had said it all.

"Want to come downstairs? Dinner will be ready soon."

"I will be down in a bit. I really want to finish this. It will drive me nuts."

Grace forced a smile. "Okay." Immediately after she left the room but before her foot even reached the top of the staircase the haunting sound of the vacuum turned back on.

~ ~ ~

Dinner that night was filled with small talk that came to an abrupt end when the conversation landed in Oliver's court. Grace forced a loving smile; Jack didn't vocalize his frustration though he also didn't attempt to hide it from his face. Oliver stared at his plate as he ate quickly in order to be excused and Hannah was enough of a talker to carry on her own conversation. A show for the entire table.

Later in the night, as Hannah lay asleep in her bed, cuddling a pink-and-purple stuffed unicorn, Jack and Grace lay wide awake staring up at the ceiling trying to tune out the dreadful sound of the vacuum flooding from Oliver's room.

# Stella and Simon

The sun rose over the small Oklahoma town. It was already a warm morning and bound to be a hot summer day; you could tell because the smell of the grass was heightened as the early sun evaporated the morning dew. The fresh, crisp air flowed through the sky and made its way into the window of a tiny, quaint one-bedroom apartment that sat at the corner of Rose and Sweetwater Boulevards.

The walls of the tiny apartment kitchen were an Easter yellow and the living room a soft pink. The colors together, though not everyone's cup of tea, were uplifting to Stella. Every time she looked at those walls, she was reminded of her favorite summer treat, a dish of strawberry and banana ice cream with a sugar cone placed on top, and it was enough to make her smile.

Stella was a special kind of soul. She could find joy in the simplest of things like the fact that today was a very special day. Today she turned nineteen and a half and she was certainly going to celebrate. She was just as gorgeous on the inside as she was on the outside. She had long, wavy brown hair with honey highlights, big brown eyes, plump lips, an olive complexion and beautiful curves. She grew up in foster care, bouncing around from one home to another until her eighteenth birthday when she aged out of the system. Though she never knew her parents she felt an empowering connection to nature and truly considered herself a daughter of the earth. She was a very spiritual young lady, wise beyond her years as well, who, despite her less than perfect upbringing, chose to radiate positive energy and quickly became an emblem of light wherever she went.

Every morning, Stella would wake up with the sun, give thanks through prayer and meditate in her sacred space. Her sacred space was a quaint corner of her baby pink living room, which was designed to follow the guidelines of feng shui. It consisted of a comfy pillow, soft blanket, reiki-charged candles, crystals, an altar with flowers, incense, a Himalayan salt lamp, and a musical device that played soothing music; the kind in which the vibrations of the sound waves danced through the cells, cleansing the body.

This morning was no different than the others. Stella sat on the floor, spine straight, legs crossed, and her hands gently resting on each knee. Next to her sat her furry companion, Simon, a handsome black cat. This was no ordinary cat. He was incredibly sociable and very chatty; he never hid, followed her around the house, and slept in her bed, sometimes on the pillow and other times under the sheets, but most unusual was the fact that not once did he miss a morning meditation. It was safe to say that he was a unique cat, just like Stella was a unique presence in the Oklahoman town. Simon's and Stella's paths had crossed by fate; he was a stray cat, stranded alone in a storm, and she, newly eighteen, was fresh out of the system and officially on her own. Instantly they were two peas in a pod. She was grateful for his companionship and often thanked the spirits for intertwining their existence.

Simon's eyes opened and closed slightly as the morning meditation wound down. Stella placed her hands in front of her heart in prayer position and bowed her head. "Namaste." She took a moment to bask in the gratitude then opened her eyes. She laughed when she saw Simon next to her, sitting tall and blinking twice as he woke up from his own meditative state. "Good boy," she said as she stroked him from his head to his tail then stood up to begin her day.

~ ~ ~

Stella danced in the shower as she lathered up her body with a vanilla-scented shower scrub on a bright aqua loofa. Simon sat on the toilet lid placing his paw into the space between the shower curtain and the wall trying to catch some of the water droplets as they fell from the shower head. Stella noticed his paw retract and reenter. She smiled as she playfully popped her head outside of the curtain. Simon meowed as he stood up on his hind legs to properly greet her with sandpaper kisses.

She turned off the water, wrapped herself in a yellow daisy woven towel and stepped out of the shower. She wiped the steam from the mirror in a circular motion just enough so she could see her face. As childish as this was it was one of her favorite things do. She patted her face with rose water and began to brush her teeth.

Once dressed, she grabbed a fresh pot of coffee and poured it into a stainless steel travel mug. She went through her checklist: "Purse, keys, phone… Okay, we're good to go." Stella walked swiftly towards the door then abruptly turned around and walked back to the window. Simon sat on the windowsill, ears alert, pupils dilated. She leaned over and gave him a kiss on the top of his head. "Bye baby. Go get those birds."

Simon meowed and went back to the hunt.

Stella grabbed her coffee mug and walked out the door.

~ ~ ~

She worked at a Bed and Bath store at the local strip mall. She worked only four days a week, which turned out to be slightly less than full time, but she didn't care. She wasn't trying to spend her life on the clock. As long as she could provide her basic needs and maybe a couple bucks to play with, she was happy.

Within seconds of her entering the store, her somewhat neurotic manager Doug came rushing up to her. His words flew from his mouth a mile a minute. "Good morning, Stella. We need you in bedding today."

Stella couldn't help but smile at him.

Sure, some of the staff made fun of the constant urgency in his delivery and complained that he was beyond strict and took his retail job way too seriously, but Stella had a soft spot for Doug. One year ago, when she had to get her tonsils extracted, Doug would find her in the store every hour and check on her well-being, just to makes sure she was doing okay. Despite his uber professional behavior Stella knew that he not only cared about his job and the company he worked for but he also cared deeply for his employees.

"Sounds good, Doug. I'll just put my stuff down and head right over."

"Thank you!" Doug exclaimed as though she was doing him a huge favor.

Stella stood proudly in the bedding section in her khaki pants, white short-sleeve button up and blue vest. Scanner gun in hand, she scanned each item on the shelf into the system. Suddenly two tiny rascals charged towards her and wrapped their arms around her.

"Stella!" the kids shouted.

"Hey guys. What a nice surprise!" Stella said as she picked them up and spun them around in circles.

The kids giggled and it was music to Stella's ears. Geri and Ryan were six-year-old freckled and ginger twins who belonged to her best friend in the whole world. They were happy kids but full of energy and at times a handful. "Where's your mom?" Stella asked.

"She's slow," Ryan said.

"Daddy said she's having a meltdown," Geri chimed in.

"Is that so?" Stella replied as the children's feet were placed back on the floor. Geri adorably nodded yes and beamed a mischievous smile, as she twirled her cherry candy sucker from one cheek to the other.

Exhausted and out of breath, Julie approached the scene, her long blonde hair in a messy ponytail; she wore a light pair of mom jeans and a disheveled white blouse where part of her cleavage was on display as she must have missed a button when she got ready that morning.

"Only a mild meltdown," Julie said as the kids screeched and took off down the aisle. "Hi," she added.

Stella gave her a much needed hug. Julie closed her eyes and damn near collapsed in her arms. She was taller than Stella and almost ten years her senior, but they had been best friends for the last three years.

The two met under a bingo tent at the county fair the summer Stella moved to the town and had been each other's rock ever sense. Julie acted as a mentor for Stella and Stella considered her to be a big sister. She genuinely loved Julie and her family.

"Can you believe it? Kyle is trying to convince me to have another one."

"Well, they are adorable angels." Stella may have spoken too soon as Geri and Ryan smacked each other with new store pillows, which didn't look so new now with the crisp plastic sleeve dragging on the ground.

"One was enough. But twins? I blame Kyle. They're on his side, not mine." Julie let out a vocal sigh of frustration. She was getting near the end of her rope. "It's been one heck of a day. Once again, I got nothing done. It's already three in the afternoon and I'm exhausted and ready for bed."

"Then I'm guessing it's safe to say you're not coming tonight?"

Julie looked at Stella with confusion. She didn't remember making any plans for that evening. She searched a bit deeper in her memory then all of a sudden dropped her jaw. "Oh my gosh, honey, your half birthday! I completely forgot. I'm so sorry," Julie apologized. "I feel like such an asshole."

"Don't. It's okay, really."

"Do you hate me?"

"Come on, I could never hate you." And she meant it. "Besides, it's not even a real birthday."

"This is true. You are the only person I know who makes it a point to celebrate a six-month marker."

Stella let out a whimsical laugh. "Well, why not add a little bit more celebration into this joyous thing called life?"

Julie's face scrunched. "Are you being sarcastic?"

"No."

"Right. I should have known that." Julie knew that Stella had an unparalleled love of life. She, on the other hand, was still questioning the universe and its ways. Julie forcefully lifted her tired face into a cheerful smile when out of nowhere a gigantic noise erupted and an entire shelf stocked with seen-on-TV merchandise came crashing to the floor. Every patron in the entire store turned their head towards the commotion. Doug dramatically grabbed his chest at the sight of the new merchandise scattered across the floor. The ability to process the situation on hand was proving difficult for him. Julie and Stella turned to see the twins caught red-handed, with guilt spread across their faces as they stood frozen next to the destruction.

"Jesus, I can't take them anywhere. We have to go before I slap the sugar out of them." Julies leaned in for a hug. "I love you."

"I love you too."

"Geri, Ryan, pick it up! Don't make me ask you twice!" Julie wailed as she walked over to them. She turned to Doug and apologized profusely. "I'm so sorry. Really." Doug nodded in a customer service understanding, trying hard to keep his composure.

# Twenty an Hour

Oliver sat at his gray desk. He had an intense focus as he carefully unwrapped his new art supplies: various sizes of charcoal pencils, a brand-new eraser and a pearl-white blending stump. He carefully placed every tool in its designated spot, then double and triple-checked their position.

Breakfast had been served at the Roads' house, blueberry pancakes and scrambled eggs, but after not seeing Oliver all morning Grace decided it was time to see what he was up to.

"Hi," she said as she entered his room.

Oliver looked over at her with a smile on his face. "Hey Mom."

Grace adored seeing his smile. It was a genuine one too this time. Lord knows he wouldn't fake a smile to please anyone. Wouldn't even fake one for the family Christmas photo. Grace was reminded of that every time her eyes caught a glimpse of the previous year's family photo that was politely displayed on one of the shelves in his room. There she, Jack, and Hannah looked happy, like one of those families from the Lands' End magazines. And then there Oliver was next to them, standing tall with his hands behind his back and his head slightly tilted downward. No smile, no emotion. Grace looked at the photo and couldn't understand why he liked it so much. *He must like it, right? Otherwise why would he display it on the shelf?* she wondered. Something about that photo sparked a heartwarming reaction in Grace. Without thinking twice, she reached out and touched the edge of the frame.

Oliver's eye caught a glimpse of her hand reaching for the photo and he quickly jumped out of his chair and rushed over to her. "Mom, don't touch that!" he barked.

Grace pulled back her hand and apologized, though she didn't understand why. Oliver shook off her apology as he rotated the frame a centimeter over, back to its designated spot. He began to calm down.

"It's okay," he said, "it just took me a while to get them all in the right place."

Then Oliver went back to his desk. He pulled out the chair and took a seat squirming ever so slightly back and forth until he felt comfortable.

Grace almost forgot why she had come into his room in the first place. When she remembered, a sigh of relief fell across her demeanor. Finally, they could change the subject. "Hannah and I are going to the store to explore the town a little and pick up some furnishings. Did you want to come with us?" she asked.

"No thanks."

"You sure? It would be nice to get out of the house for a bit. Don't you think?"

"I want to finish setting up my room." Oliver looked down and noticed a tiny piece of plastic wrap that looked like it came from the packaging of his new charcoal kit. He picked the piece up off the floor. "Plus, I have to vacuum this rug again. It's not right." His eyes scanned the rug for the umpteenth time.

Moments went by and Oliver could feel his mother's concerned stare. He looked Grace straight in the eye, which was rare. "Seriously Mom, I'm fine. You guys have fun."

Grace nodded in understanding. As she left the room, she saw Oliver wander back to the shelf and adjust the picture frame once more. One half centimeter to the left.

~ ~ ~

Grace and Hannah had a wonderful mother-daughter day. They drove through the town admiring the flat farmland, beautiful pastures, and the kindness of the natives. They bought some cushions for their patio furniture, navy blue with a pattern of yellow tulips floating about. Next, they made a stop at the park where Hannah met some new friends. She and the other kids played on the jungle gym for hours. They even taught her a new game called Lava, which she enjoyed very much. The kids stopped their game only once to ask their parents for money to buy treats from the ice cream truck that drove past the park every day precisely at two o'clock in the afternoon, blaring that catchy tune. The adults obliged and joined in with a treat of their own.

Grace got along great with the other parents. Their kids were very well mannered. "Pleases," "Thank yous" and "yes ma'ams" all around. She was impressed. The more Grace saw of Oklahoma the more she could see them all being happy here. The folks were simple, kind, inviting, hospitable, and seemed to treat even a stranger like they would a grand old friend.

~　~　~

Day turned to evening. The sun was beginning to set, which created a blinding beam of light. Grace and Jack sat on the couch watching television, a glass of Chardonnay in her hand and a Scotch on the rocks for him. Jack's arm was securely stretched out and rested over Grace's shoulder. He had a way of making her always feel comforted and protected in his presence. There wasn't anything he wouldn't do for his family and she knew it.

They heard Oliver tiptoe down the steps, walk towards the kitchen and head straight to the refrigerator.

"Hey." Grace felt her voice go up an octave. "What are you working on up there?"

"Nothing, just some scratch sketches. They're all crap. No inspiration here."

"Well, Hannah went next door to play SPUD with the neighbor kids. I'm sure you can join them. Maybe some fresh air or making some new friends will spark some inspiration," Grace suggested, like any mother would.

Oliver knew his mother tried her hardest to make him "feel better" or whatever, but he felt fine. He was fine. Besides, he thought a game called SPUD sounded childish. Though he didn't know anything about the game he knew that he didn't want to play with the neighbor kids and that he was perfectly fine spending his time inside, alone in his room.

"No thanks," he replied then simply walked back up the stairs.

Jack could see the sorrow in Grace's eyes as she watched Oliver climb the stairs. When she heard the door slam, she closed her eyes and took a deep breath in and out.

"That's it," Jack said as he abruptly rose from the couch.

Grace immediately opened her eyes with concern. "Wait Jack, please don't," she begged.

"Grace, it will be fine. I can talk to my son."

Before she could protest any further Jack was already up the stairs. He seemed to be on a mission. He barged through the closed door to Oliver's room. Oliver didn't even flinch; he just turned his head, noticed Jack standing tall in front of him, and went back to his sketches.

"Look Oliver, I know that you didn't want to move here but none of us really had a choice in that matter. So instead of isolating yourself in this room, drawing circles and organizing … stuff … can you do us a favor?" Jack reached into his pocket, pulled out a twenty-dollar bill from his wallet and held it out to his son. "Here, just take this and go out on the town for an hour. I don't care if you go buy a cup of coffee, a chocolate bar from the gas station or deposit it into a savings account. Humor us. Okay? Because locking yourself in this room is upsetting your mother." He added, "And me."

Oliver stared at the twenty-dollar bill that his father held out with desperation written all over his face. Seconds went by and time seemed to freeze over. Jack blinked for a moment. He caught a glimpse of how absurd his notion was, but he was stubborn, and he didn't know what else to do so he wouldn't budge. He couldn't budge. Oliver briefly looked into his father's eyes and spotted a quick glimpse of uncertainty.

Oliver wondered how his father could be so wrong about the situation. Oliver didn't care if he was stuck in this small Oklahoman town, back in Boulder or the city before that one, or the city before that. No matter what city he was in he would be doing the same thing. Staying in his room. Minding his own business.

His room was his space and his parents didn't understand how one could be perfectly content in their own space. He felt comfortable in his room; the posters of the legends on his wall inspired him to dream, the more he dreamed the more he could live amongst them. His sketches were an outlet, an opportunity to release all the thoughts, stresses, and nuisances that constantly sprinted through his head. When he drew, his restless mind was finally at peace.

"Oliver!" Jack screeched. Sometimes he could be intimidating. Scary even.

Oliver rose abruptly, snatched the twenty from his father's hands and reached for the light gray sweatshirt that was draped over the back of his chair. He clenched his teeth as he grunted, "Don't touch my stuff." Then Oliver sharply maneuvered around his father's stance.

Jack's face relaxed for a moment. "Thank you," he mumbled under his breath.

Oliver's feet stomped like a bull in a china shop as he sprinted down the stairs.

"Where are you going?" Grace shouted after him.

"Out," he said sharply. "I'll be back in fifty-nine minutes and twenty-four seconds." Then he slammed the front door shut.

Grace sat on the couch, shocked and a bit confused. She saw Jack walk slowly down the stairs regaining his composure with every step. "What did you say to him?" she questioned with anger at the base of her tone.

Jack took a moment to answer. It was clear that the encounter had him a bit shaken as well. "Don't worry about it," he said. "I just talked some sense into him." He dropped his head; his eyes blinked a few times as if he was trying to bring himself back to reality.

Jack loved his son, he just didn't understand him. Jack came from a large family, four brothers and one sister, six kids in total. His mom was as sweet as could be, which was important because his father would be quick to crack the whip. Their opposites created balance in the household. His father had to be strict, especially when raising five boys, there was no other way to calm the testosterone. In his childhood home the ability to be an alpha male was praised. Tough love was how his father showed affection and it worked. All of his siblings, including Jack, grew up to live a more than comfortable life, but more importantly they all had created wonderful families of their own.

Jack wanted what was best for his kids, just like his parents wanted the same for him. He just couldn't understand why Oliver still insisted on living with them. Jack moved out the day he turned eighteen. It's a milestone in life that most teens can't wait to hit. He could still vividly hear his father say, "I raised you till you were eighteen, I did my job; now you do yours. Go, live and pay for your own damn self." Jack laughed when he thought of this. His dad, may he in rest in peace, was a bit rough around the edges but he raised six kids who all went on to live fulfilling lives; therefore most people would say he did a good job.

Oliver was nineteen years old, he graduated high school at seventeen, never went to one prom, homecoming, sports games, or anything of the sort. He took all advanced placement classes and passed them with flying colors. His father made him apply to top universities and he got into all of them—Yale, Princeton, MIT—but he didn't want to go. Jack was prepared to pay the hefty tuition for an outstanding college education. He was proud of his son and had been setting aside money for his kid's college fund for years, preparing for this very moment. He couldn't fathom why Oliver had passed on all of them only to attend the state university, which allowed him to live at home. He thought, This must be a joke, and almost let out a tirade of anger, but Grace had pulled him back.

"Let him do what he wants," she said. "Besides, you may be the only parent who complains about not paying such a hefty tuition."

Jack knew that Grace had more patience with Oliver than he did. She had noticed their son's unusual habits early on. He was in first grade when she started volunteering to help with his class. While the other kids played together at recess Oliver would sit by himself, and if some energized child came over to play with him, he would simply drop the toy from his hand, move to an adjacent corner and begin to play with something else.

As he grew older, she realized his mildly obsessive behavior had started to develop further. He was neat, very neat, and his attention to detail was remarkable.

When he was in third grade, Grace was called into the principal's office. She rushed into the school with her nails still wet from the salon. She was frantic. "What is it? Is he okay? What's going on?" she demanded.

The principal calmly gestured to the chair across from her desk. "How about you take a seat, Mrs. Roads?"

Grace obliged.

"Mrs. Roads," began the principal, "your son is fine. In fact, we called you in because the students were painting in art class today. They each had the freedom to paint whatever they felt drawn to."

Grace scrunched her face, unable to predict where this was going and why this required her presence.

The principal continued, "While most of the students' artwork looked like blobs of scattered paint, Oliver's … well … he drew this." The principal held out a medium-sized canvas.

Grace's jaw dropped as she studied the painting. She reached out and pulled the canvas closer. "Oh my," she said in a state of shock.

"Exactly my thoughts," said the principal.

Oliver had painted three blue jays playing in a cobblestone bird bath surrounded by long strands of overgrown grass. There was a tiny lady bug on one of the blades of grass and an overcast sky of gray stratus clouds. Grace could see that this wasn't just a child's art project, this was a beautiful portrait. Her son had a talent, a God-given gift. She smiled.

"In my fifteen years of working with kids I have never seen such talent. Where did he even come up with an idea like that?" the principal asked.

"It's the view from my mother's patio," said Grace. She didn't know how Oliver had retained the details of that view. They saw her mother once a year, maybe twice on a rare occasion, and Oliver was just a child. An observant child clearly. But how did he store it into his memory? She couldn't comprehend it.

"Mrs. Roads, this goes without saying, but your son is extremely gifted in the arts. This might be something worth pursuing."

Grace looked up at the principal. "Of course. Thank you for sharing with me. It's okay if I keep this," she stated rather than asked.

"Certainly."

Grace exited the principal's office holding the canvas tightly and close to her heart. Oliver sat in the hallway. He looked up at his mother. "Am I in trouble?"

"Not at all, sweetheart. You're a genius."

"What's a genius?" he innocently asked.

Grace smiled.

They stopped at the art supply store on their way home where she let Oliver pick out fifty dollars' worth of supplies. His face lit up and for the first time in a long time she saw a real smile appear across her young son's face.

When they arrived home, she immediately hung the canvas on the wall in the living room and waited for Jack to come home so she could share with him the events of the day. When Jack arrived, she beamed with pride as she told him about her meeting with the principal. She then showed him the beautiful painting. Jack looked at it for a couple seconds and nodded. "Not bad," he said.

"Not bad? Honey, he's an artistic genius. Like van Gogh or Picasso."

Jack chuckled. "Okay, if you say so." He walked away.

But Grace did say so. That day, all of Jack's plans for Oliver to follow in his footsteps and become an athletic protégé went right out the window. Grace took Jack's sarcastic, "Okay, if you say so," as a complete agreement that he would pursue the arts, if or until he changed his mind on his own merit. Jack wasn't worried. He was convinced that it was a phase. One that Oliver was sure to grow out of once high school came around and sports and girls waltzed into the picture. But he was wrong; high school came but Oliver's focus never wavered. Though it seemed unlikely that Oliver was going to change his interests Jack still maintained hope. Oliver had not one friend and seemed to spend all his time by himself. To an outside observer he was a unique kid quietly staring at the wall. But in his own reality he was living a life through his imagination. His hobbies included cleaning and drawing and living in his own world.

~   ~   ~

Back at their new house, a now composed Jack took a seat next to his wife.

"Are you okay?" she asked.

Jack nodded followed by a sigh of frustration. "I can't wait for this phase to be over," he said. "I just don't understand it."

Grace placed her head on his shoulder. She loved her husband and she knew he loved Oliver just as much as she did, but she wondered when he was going to realize that this wasn't a phase. This was who Oliver was.

# The Dreslen Piano Bar

Oliver walked one foot in front of the other at a steady pace, releasing frustration with every step, and within a couple blocks he reached the start of the downtown area, if you could even call it that. The town was small to begin with. This place they referred to as a downtown area was really just a single street. It was less than a mile long with a grand church on one end and the fairgrounds on the other. Old cream stone buildings built in the eighteen hundreds, many embellished with the charm of climbing vines and ivy, lined each side of the street. There was a town hall with a grand clock, a single bank, a single park, a single dentist, a single movie theatre, two bars, several antique shops and an overkill of coffee houses.

Oliver walked down the street minding his own business. He watched as his foot tapped the sidewalk, careful not to lay a foot on a crack, when suddenly he came to an abrupt stop after hearing the faint sound of a piano scale. He took two steps back, turned to the left and found himself standing in front of a tiny wooden door, hidden by giant, uninviting, overgrown, green vines. Above the door was a rustic vintage lantern that let off a golden hue. The door was slightly ajar, and the music continued to play. Oliver stood in silence debating his next move when before he could make a decision his curiosity took over and he found himself entering the mysterious establishment.

Oliver walked through the secret wooden door, which led to a short and snug brick hallway. From there he turned a sharp corner and was met by three rickety steps, which brought him to a snug cellar that led him to the bar of The Dreslen. A look of awe and wonderment swept across his face. The Dreslen was much more spacious than the entry way advertised. It felt like you were walking into a time warp, a speakeasy, a world of its own. It had stone cobbled floors and solid brick walls. There was a long bar to his right and another across the way both made with a deep oak wood and the venue was dimly illuminated by unique, industrial-looking chandeliers made from wire, upside down glass bottles and miniature bulbs. There was a raised platform in the center of the room meant to act as a stage and on that platform sat two beautiful, sleek black pianos. The pianos faced each other and were each equipped with a vintage Western Electric microphone that hung straight down from the ceiling.

The Dreslen had no patrons, only staff, all hustling to prepare for the night. The servers were dressed in black slacks, matching button-down shirts and maroon bow ties. They quickly set each circular table with black cloth covers, a water glass, an appetizer plate, a roll up, and, last but not least, an oil-burning candle. With the help of the hostess they pushed tables together in order to accommodate the large party reservations for the evening while the bartenders counted their banks and the barbacks were busy polishing glasses and preparing for the night.

Ethan, a barback similar in age to Oliver, walked quickly across the floor with a giant bucket of ice in his hands. En route he passed Oliver and without stopping said in his authentic Australian accent, "Hey mate. We open in like ten minutes, for the time being you can sit wherever you want. The host will be with you shortly." He walked behind the bar, bent slightly at his knees then hoisted the heavy ice filled bucket and emptied its contents into the well. Oliver stepped up to the bar.

"What's going on here?"

Ethan looked up at him. He wiped a glistening bead of sweat from his brows as his sandy blond locks began to curl. He studied his presence and he knew that look. It was the look he had when he first ran into the mysterious Dreslen Piano Bar. It was clear to Ethan that Oliver was a transplant to these parts. Just like him. He said cheerfully, "It's Thursday night at The Dreslen Piano Bar, what do you think?"

Oliver shrugged his shoulders.

"Dueling pianos, mate!" Ethan grabbed the ice bucket off the floor and went back to the kitchen to fill it up again. On his way, he shouted once more, "Give it a stay for a bit. This place … it's magical!"

At that moment Oliver heard, "Can I get more volume please and a diet cola?"

He turned and noticed the voice came from a man dressed to the nines in a black tuxedo with a classic tailcoat, accessorized with a deep purple pocket square and a felt bowler hat. Wrinkles of joyous life outlined the gentleman's face as he sat up straight on the piano bench. He clasped his hands together intertwining his fingers, let out multiple cracks of release and then gently placed his fingers on the keys. From the looks of the gentleman you would have expected him to play a slow, soothing jazz or a ballad, but this was not the case. In the blink of an eye his fingers jumped from one key to another. They moved so quickly it was impossible to keep up. It was as though each finger got a jolt of adrenaline and was taking its spike of energy out on the keys. He played a couple measures and ended with a mesmerizing glissando. His smile lit up the dim room. It was almost as though the sound of the music sent his soul back to the excitement of his youth. Music can do that, it's powerful enough to send one on a journey. Every time he was blessed to take the stage, he felt young again. "Ya hear that?" He laughed. "I still got it!"

Delighted by this man's joy, Oliver made his way over to a small table set for two in the far corner of the room. This was an ideal table. It was on the outskirts of the room and close to a wall making it feel slightly more private. Yet there was still a nice view of the stage. He noticed a tiny place holder set on the table that read,

"Reserved." He wasn't one to break the rules, so he looked around to see if there was another table in an equally prime location.

Ethan walked across the room again, carrying another bucket of ice. He noticed Oliver and shouted, "You can sit there. The reservation isn't until way later."

Oliver draped his jacket over the chair. He took a seat and admired the ambience. Much to his surprise he felt comfortable there. It was a feeling he couldn't explain. But he liked it.

# A Happy Half Birthday

It was almost the end of Stella's eight-hour shift. This day flew by; perhaps it was the excitement for that evening's half birthday festivities. Even though Julie couldn't celebrate with her, Stella still planned on carrying out the evening. She didn't mind going to places by herself. She also realized that a half birthday celebration wouldn't be understood by most, so it became a tradition she kept to herself, but Julie, being an exceptionally caring friend, thought a half birthday sounded fun and had gladly joined in the festivities for the past few years.

Julie and Stella had a wonderful friendship. Over the years Julie had confided in Stella about her journey through motherhood and about the struggles she was having. "One never knows what it's like to be a mother," she said. "Your entire life changes. I worry constantly; they piss me off, they get under my skin, they cost a fortune... They also make me laugh and exuberate love from my heart that I didn't even know existed. They truly are the pain in my ass, the light in my life, and a reason to wake up in the morning all wrapped into one ... well, two." She laughed. "It's a trip." Stella couldn't help but laugh whenever she remembered this conversation. She knew that Julie loved being a mom but she also could see that she needed to take care of herself and if that meant missing her half birthday, she was perfectly okay with it.

Stella finished dressing one of the model beds on the floor in a new comforter design, white with bright orange and yellow swirls. Too kid-like for some, but she loved it. It reminded her of the sun. She fluffed the pillows and picked up the plastic packaging from off the floor. Suddenly Doug appeared behind her. "All done?" he asked.

"Yep!"

Doug looked at his watch. There was still a good half hour left on her shift. "Why don't you take off early?" he suggested.

"Really?" She couldn't disguise the excitement in her voice.

"Yes, thanks for coming in today. You did good work."

"Thanks, Doug. I'll see you next week." Stella began to walk away.

"And Stella," he chimed in, "happy half birthday."

"How did you—"

"Your friend told me. The one with the—" his face cringed for a moment "—cute kids."

Stella laughed. "Well, thank you, Doug." She then walked out of the store like she always did … with a pep in her step.

~ ~ ~

Hours later, Stella entered The Dreslen. She wore a beautiful red dress that rested above her knees simply paired with strappy black sandals with a slightly elevated heel. Her long hair was in loose curls pinned back behind the right ear and secured in place with a red rose.

The place was packed, wine was poured, and the dueling pianos were going at it, taking their audience on a grand adventure. Stella loved The Dreslen because it was unique and unexplained. It was a place that no one would expect a town like this to have, which is why it was so perfect in her eyes. She'd stumbled upon The Dreslen Piano Bar a couple years ago when she first moved to town. She was eager and excited to explore the town and ended up finding this hidden gem. She was also young and the first time she came to The Dreslen she was sure they would kick her out, but they never checked IDs, nor was this a place where people came to drink. They came to enjoy a show and therefore Stella was welcome. For the first few months she came almost every night after work. She got to know the entire staff and quickly became a seasoned regular. Though now she didn't come by as often as she used to, they were still always happy to see her smiling face. The staff felt like family to her. Whenever she popped in unexpectedly, even if it was just to say hi, she was greeted with open arms. It was like no time had passed.

Stella walked over to the bar where she saw Ethan. "Hey stranger," she said.

Ethan looked up. "Stella! Oh my gosh!" he exclaimed as he rushed out from behind the bar, picked her up and swung her through the air. "Happy half birthday, you crazy … I mean spiritual angel of light," he joked. "It's so good to see you," he said as he put her down and gave her one final twirl and a friendly hug. "You look gorgeous."

Stella was all smiles and giggles. Ethan had such magnetic, playful energy. One she admired. Unfortunately, the moment was cut short when the bartender snapped, "Ethan, we're swamped! I need you back here washing glasses."

Ethan nodded at the bartender. "Copy that!" He then looked over to Stella. "I've got to go back. The glamorous work awaits," he teased. "Oh, we have a table reserved for you," he said as he pointed to a small table across the way.

Stella looked over to the table. She noticed a young man, curly hair, dark-framed glasses, jeans and a dark T-shirt sitting contently and alone at her table. "Ethan, why is there a man at my table?" she asked.

Ethan looked over and saw Oliver still seated at the table. "Oh shoot, I didn't know he was still here. He's been here since we opened. Give me a second, I'll ask him to move."

"No, it's okay," Stella jumped in. "It's just me tonight anyway. I don't mind the company."

"You sure?"

"Yeah."

"Ethan!" the bartender snapped.

Ethan ran behind the bar. "Enjoy the night!"

Stella made her way across the crowded room and landed at her table. She tapped the gentleman on the shoulder. He jumped, a bit alarmed. "Sorry, I didn't mean to scare you."

Oliver insisted she didn't scare him, he was just startled. He had been so swept away in the music that the unexpected shoulder tap shocked him back into reality. He turned to see a very, very stunning young lady in red. He didn't know what to say, was she lost? *Why on earth would she be talking to me?* he pondered. His mind was flooded with negative and demoralizing chatter. And then she spoke a simple phrase.

"This is my table," she said apologetically as she pointed to the reserved sign.

Oliver hopped up and hastily grabbed his sweatshirt. "Sorry, sorry. I saw the sign; they said it was okay, but I lost track of time, I've been here awhile. Sorry, I'm sorry." He took a breath.

"Oh, no, it's okay. I didn't mean it like that, more like that's the reason why this random girl is going to join your table."

Stella smiled sincerely. At that moment the stage lights shifted, and the light lit her up. Oliver noticed the ruby on her lips and for a split second the demoralizing chatter in his mind stopped. *Wow*, he thought, *that shade really complements her complexion.*

"Please stay."

Again, he was struck back into reality, "No, ah … no."

"I insist. It's just me anyway."

Oliver stood in silence for what felt like an eternity until she spoke again. "Please?" she asked.

Oliver was immensely confused, his palms were sweaty. Her stare seemed much more intense than it should have been, and he didn't know what the right response was. Quite frankly he didn't even know if his legs would work if he chose to walk away; would he make it out the door or were they going to give out momentarily and he'd soon be on the ground? He couldn't remember when he stopped feeling them, but it was sometime during this encounter. "Okay," he heard himself say. He took his seat; probably the safer bet. Stella followed suit.

"I'm Stella."

"Oliver."

Her face lit up. "Like Oliver Twist!"

"Yeah ... sure."

The waitress approached the table. Oliver was relieved.

"Drinks?" she asked.

"I'll have a cab, please." Stella smiled.

Oliver pointed to his empty glass. "One more, please."

The waitress's eyes slightly gave shade as she walked away.

"What are you drinking?" Stella enquired.

"Club soda."

"Wild," she teased.

"I don't drink."

Stella pulled back. "Oh, too much partying in your college years?"

"No, underage."

Stella leaned in. "Me too. You must be new to town."

Oliver couldn't understand why she insisted on keeping a conversation going. He wasn't trying to end the conversation by any means, but most people took his one-word answers, less than enthusiastic delivery and lack of eye contact as an assumption that chatting with him was going to be a waste of their time. But this girl for whatever reason wasn't backing down. "Why do you say I'm new?" he asked.

"It's a really small town. Everyone pretty much knows everyone. Plus, I haven't seen you around. I would have remembered you." Her words landed with confidence.

Oliver turned his head slightly away from her. "Oh," he said. The thoughts in his head became overbearing. *What's up with this girl? Why would she have remembered you? I bet it's because you're weird.* His anxiety was at an all-time high, higher than it had been in a long time.

Stella noticed his knee start to frantically bounce up and down under the table. She reached out her hand and placed it gently on his kneecap, bringing it to a halt. "Am I making you nervous?" she asked.

"Huh?" For the third time that night, she brought him out of his mind and back to reality. It must be a weird superpower of hers, he thought. Before he could gather control, the words poured out of his mouth. "Ah, no, I'm fine. Just a little anxious, a tad OCD, anti-social, awkward and weird mixed into one."

Stella waited a moment before responding. This was the most he'd said in the same breath since they met. She was pleasantly caught off guard. "At least you are self-aware. Even if you are a little … unique."

*Unique*, he thought. *That's never a good word.*

She let out a flirtatious giggle before continuing. "Relax. Being unique is not a bad thing. I like that about you. I'm a little unusual too. You're in good company."

Somehow Oliver gained the courage to look at Stella. Their eyes locked and for the first time in his life time he felt a flutter in his stomach. There, right in front of his eyes, engaging in conversation with him was an alluring, charming woman who seemed to be just as perfect on the inside as she was on the outside—kind, understanding, inviting and weird, just like him.

He felt her sincerity when she spoke and her smile was not only comforting, joyous and full of life but also contagious. Before Oliver could process the thoughts sprouting in his mind, his body beat him to it. He smiled a real smile back at her.

# A Night at The Dreslen

The musical keys of the pianos continued to play into the night. Stella and Oliver exchanged a few words here and there, but both of them were perfectly pleased to say very little and instead get lost in the music. Every once in a while, Oliver would glance over at Stella to make sure she hadn't become irritated or annoyed by his presence. Plus it didn't hurt to have a reminder that this very attractive woman, and a peer, was sharing a table with him and didn't seem to loathe it.

Stella swayed back and forth in her chair. Occasionally she would close her eyes and feel the vibrations rush through her body. Her face exuberated freedom, and this freedom intrigued Oliver. Something about her company made him feel good. He couldn't explain why or how, but for the first time in a long time his anxiety started to subdue. She caught him staring every once in a while, which made his heart beat a little faster. *Thank God it's dark in here*, he thought, *I'm blushing galore*. Instead of making a big deal about it she just smiled at him and turned her focus back to the music.

~ ~ ~

Before he knew it, the night was over. As the audience clapped, Oliver took a glance at his wristwatch. It was already ten thirty at night. He'd definitely surpassed his one-hour sentence and, much to his surprise, wasn't ready to call it a night.

Stella leaned in. "Did you love it?"

"It was awesome!"

"They do the dueling pianos the first Thursday of every month, if you're ever interested in coming again."

"Definitely."

Stella grabbed her purse, Oliver grabbed his jacket and the two headed towards the exit. "Aw, people in love. I love that," Stella said as they passed the bar.

Oliver didn't know what she was referring to until he looked over his shoulder and saw three patrons at the bar. One man and two women. Their hands were all over one another, clearly an enjoyable end to their evening. "Just looks like they're drunk," Oliver stated.

"Maybe." Her face lit up. "Or maybe they're in love."

"The three of them?" he said in disbelief.

"Yeah, maybe the three of them actually love one another," she proposed with confidence.

"I don't think so."

"Why not?" Stella was both curious and entertained.

"'Cause it's hard enough for two people to love each other, could you imagine how many elements would have to come together for three?'"

Stella let out a giggle. She couldn't tell if he meant it as a joke or truly believed it. Either way her first impression of him was proving to be right, he was special, unique, and so was she.

They walked outside and were greeted by a warm, perfect summer's night garnished with a giant moon, the kind that lit up the sky. The kind that could guide one home. When Stella caught a gaze, she smiled a smile that could say so much without saying anything at all. Neither one of them were ready for the night to be over, but neither was prepared to say so either. As more patrons left the establishment, Stella and Oliver stood awkwardly outside. Oliver leaned against the side of the building. Stella folded her arms. "You're a cynic when it comes to love," she said.

"Sometimes," he admitted. "Obviously you believe in it?" he questioned, referring to the incident at the bar.

"I do," she said proudly. "I adore love."

Oliver smiled. "Ah, you're one of those."

"Yes."

"Have you ever been IN love?" he asked.

"IN love?"

"Yes," he replied, "IN love."

Stella paused for a moment. Her eyes tilted upwards as though she was looking through her brain paging through her own thoughts. "No," she finally said. Oliver couldn't help but recognize the longing in her inflection. "But I know that it exists."

"Really? How do you know?" Oliver leaned in, curious to hear her thoughts.

"I see it all the time. In the restaurants, at the movies, in the park…"As she continued to rattle off her list, he could see that she got lost purely in the idea of love and what it must feel like to experience it. "Everywhere I go," she finished.

In disbelief Oliver replied, "Huh."

She continued, "And in a sense, I guess I've experienced it."

"Have you?" he questioned, clearly amused.

Stella ignored his sarcasm. "Yes."

"Do explain." Oliver had a twinkle in his eye as he playfully poked fun. But he truly was interested to see what fueled her thoughts. He hoped she could articulate all of the emotion.

"Well, not in this lifetime, but in a past life."

It took every bone in his body not to laugh at the fairy tale coming out of her mouth. Past life was not something he believed in, but watching her speak was wonderful. It was like watching a child excited to go to bed on Christmas Eve because Santa would be coming and bringing with him a plethora of gifts. He thought the passion she spoke with was adorable. It was clear as crystal that she wholeheartedly believed and felt everything she was saying. He knew she was just as unique in her own way as he was in his and that thought alone was comforting.

Stella continued, "One day, I'm going to meet someone and it's all going to click.

Everything. The feeling is going to be so familiar, so wonderful, that it will feel like I've come home. And that's how I'll know that he's the one."

After moments of dazzling in her own dream she was brought back to reality when Oliver playfully stated, "And I thought I was the weird one."

"I'll take that as a compliment." The two shared a smile. Stella went on, "Clearly you don't believe love exists?"

"Well, I've never felt it. In this lifetime or a past one," he joked. "Besides, they say you can't truly give love to someone until you love yourself."

His words grabbed ahold of Stella. "You don't love yourself then?"

Instead of answering, he simply replied, "Do you?"

"Of course I do."

"Wow, how modest," he teased.

"Well, what's not to love?" she said with her captivating wit and charm.

Oliver laughed, a rose hue blushed his pale cheeks as he looked her straight in the eye and answered, "Nothing … you seem perfect."

For the first time all night Stella's eyes teetered. "Flaws and all?" she asked.

"Sure. Flaws and all," he confirmed.

Stella's eyes found his. "Corny," she said.

Oliver blushed again. He quickly looked away; that was too many blushes for one night.

Stella noticed and she liked that about him. He was sensitive. "Perfectly corny enough for us to be great friends. Oliver … Twist."

~  ~  ~

The night at The Dreslen, meeting Stella, having a friend, it all felt like a dream, one he never wanted to wake up from. But when he arrived at his front door it was back to reality. It was eleven fifteen when Oliver stepped in through the front door. The door slammed behind him waking Grace who lay on the couch resting her eyes as the television played in the background. "You were out late," she said.

"Sorry, I didn't know you were waiting up."

"You can ask any mother out there, we can't sleep peacefully until we know our kids are home safe." She yawned. "Did you have fun?"

"I did."

"Really?" she asked in shock. "What did you do?"

"Saw some dueling pianos. Made a friend." With that, Oliver headed towards the stairs.

"A friend?" Grace wanted more, but Oliver wasn't about to elaborate.

"Yep. Good night, Mom." He disappeared up the stairs. Grace was shortly behind him, pleasantly surprised by the evening's events.

# This Friend

Summers in Oklahoma are famously hot and the next day was no exception. It was the humidity that made it an uncomfortable day, but the rewards were those endless summer nights. If you've ever experienced a Southern summer's night, you'll know that close to dusk the air cools creating a perfect, warm environment lit by the moon instead of the sun. The beauty of nights like this makes the day's heat and humidity well worth it.

It was midday and Stella and Julie sat inside enjoying every minute of the gluttonous air conditioning courtesy of the Bed and Bath store. They both sat comfortably in the pleather display massage chairs. Stella was taking her thirty-minute break and Julie had planned to meet up with her so they could partake in some much-needed girl talk. Stella was in the middle of telling Julie all about her encounter with Oliver. "And then he shyly asked me for my number. I've never seen a man blush so much before!"

"Did you give it to him?"

"Of course I did. He was sweet." A slight pink hue graced her cheeks.

"Speaking of blushing…" Julie smiled. The girls giggled like they were kids again and Julie had caught Stella crushing on a boy.

"He texted me this morning."

"Oh! What did he text?"

"Oliver."

Julie waited for the rest of it but no words came. Her face dropped. "His name? That's it?"

"Yep."

"A man of few words. Are you going to text him back?"

"I don't know," she pondered. "That's kind of an unrespondable text, don't you think?"

Julie shrugged her shoulders as she thought for a moment. She and Kyle were high school sweethearts; it'd been a long time since she had to dissect a text from a potential suitor. "I think you should text him," she said with certainty. "You're Miss Spiritual, always saying how things happen for a reason and people enter into our lives. What do you always say? Oh yes, for a reason, a season or a lifetime. I feel like you have to explore it. Maybe meeting him was a stroke of serendipity."

Stella nodded in agreement, unable to wipe the smile from her face. "Maybe."

Julie moved her hand down the side of the chair and pressed a small button, which turned the massage chair up one level. She let out a sigh of relaxation. "This feels so good."

She spoke too soon, within seconds Geri came rushing up to Julie shouting, "Mommy, Mommy! Time to go!"

Julie opened her eyes. "Well, it was great while it lasted." She looked at Geri who stared at her, wide eyed and beaming proudly with her half-toothed smile. Julie had to admit she and Kyle made some really adorable kids, monsters but adorable. Kyle held Ryan in his arms. As they approached the girls he set Ryan down and the instant Ryan's feet touched the ground he and Geri took off down the aisle. "And you want to have another one?" Julie asked Kyle.

"But they're so cute."

"Yeah, until they start running."

Julie and Kyle made a unique pair. Kyle was a skinny, thin-framed man with a buzzed head and the beginnings of a receding hairline. He had bright blue eyes and a very distinct jaw line. He was simple and quiet. Julie was the exact opposite in every way as she was loud, opinionated, and dominant. It was clear that Julie was the alpha in their relationship and Kyle let her be; in fact, that was maybe exactly why they fell in love in the first place. Someone said opposites attract. Either way it seemed to work for them. They'd been together for almost thirteen years.

Julie stood up and gave Stella a hug. "Bye girly. Remember, dinner next week."

"I'll be there."

Julie and Kyle wrangled up the kids and exited the store. Stella, who still had about five minutes left of her break, pulled out her phone from her back pocket and texted Oliver: *Want to see a movie tonight?*

~ ~ ~

Oliver had spent the day in the air conditioning too, except he was once again in his room, vacuuming that rug. He felt his phone vibrate in his side pocket. This didn't happen often, so he was eager to see who it could be. He turned off the vacuum, reached into his pocket and read a text from Stella. He blinked a couple times to make sure his eyes weren't playing tricks on him. She wanted to go to the movies that evening, with him. He replied: *Sure.*

~ ~ ~

Great, Stella thought, another one-word text. She replied: *Great! See you at 7. Bring some enthusiasm!* Then she clocked back in and went to work.

~ ~ ~

Her text made Oliver chuckle. He slid his phone back into his side pocket and continued to vacuum until the day turned to night.

~ ~ ~

It was almost seven and even though the movie theatre was only a five-minute walk he did not want to be late. Oliver walked down the stairs in his usual jeans and a T-shirt. Grace was in the kitchen making dinner while Jack and Hannah helped set the table. Jack looked up and noticed Oliver. Aside from his attire he looked a bit different. Jack noticed that his son had run a comb through his hair at least one extra time and there was a hint of an aroma of cheap male body spray Grace had bought him nearly eight years ago when he started to go through puberty. At that time she would have done anything to mask his odor.

Grace looked up at him. "You look nice," she said, "smell good too."

"Where are you going?" Jack asked. He really was curious. Had he missed something? "Dinner's almost ready," he stated.

"To the movies," Oliver said, "with a friend."

You could have heard a pin drop onto the wooden floor. Jack's ears pricked up.

Oliver didn't care to wait for a reaction and the silence in the room was making him uncomfortable, so he left. When the door shut, Jack spoke. "Oliver has a friend?" he asked Grace.

Grace just smiled. "Mm-hmm."

"This is good," Jack said with a tone of relief. He thought to himself, *perhaps his "phase" is over.* "So … this friend?" He fished for more.

"Stella, her name is Stella." Grace said.

"It's a girl?" Jack was astonished.

"Yes."

Hannah chimed in, "Does that mean he has a girlfriend?"

Jack dialed in on Grace's response. He was just as curious as Hannah was, if not more.

"No." Grace set the record straight. "It means he has a friend who happens to be a girl."

# The Emerald City

Oliver walked past the line of cars waiting to pull into the movie theatre. It felt as though the entire town showed up that night, there was no way they would all fit into the town's single-screen theatre. As he stood outdoors by the ticket booth, he noticed a sign that read, "Drive-in Fridays; The Classics All Summer Long!" Suddenly all the cars pulling into the sizeable plot of land behind the theatre made sense. He looked around but couldn't see Stella through all the cars. "Hey!" she shouted as she made her way through the crowd of people in line for concessions.

"Wish I would have known this was a drive-in. I would have brought a car," he joked.

"Don't be silly, we don't need one."

"Huh?"

"Follow me." Stella grabbed his hand and led the way. She brought him behind the building and past the parked cars, where families were sitting on the roofs of their vehicles, popcorn in hand, patiently waiting for the film to start. The sun began to set, they had about fifteen minutes before it would be completely gone and the movie would start. Stella picked up the pace as she and Oliver began to run through a bright green pasture.

"Where are you taking me?" Oliver asked.

They came to a stop in the middle of the pasture at the base of a water tower. "Relax," she said, "we're here."

Oliver looked up at the water tower which was very, very high up in the sky. He then looked at the rusty ladder that hung down straight to eye level. This ladder was a vertical climb up the side of the pole that seemed to have held up this tower for centuries. He saw where she was going with this. He hesitated. "I don't know about this."

"You'll be fine. I do this all the time."

"It looks really unsanitary." He rubbed his pinky finger on the ladder, pulled it back and shrieked at the bronze rust that in a single touch transferred from the ladder to his finger. "Eww." He bent down and wiped his finger on the grass.

Stella sternly looked his way and demanded, "Oliver Twist, where is your sense of adventure? Come on! You don't know what you're missing." With that she grabbed hold of the ladder and hoisted herself up. She gazed back down at Oliver who was still rooted on the ground. "Come on!"

Oliver looked around the empty pasture and then back up at Stella as she quickly made progress on the ladder. He tried to think about what would be worse, climbing up a water tower on a rusty ladder or stuck in a vacant pasture when the night came. His mind began to race with paranoid thoughts, he'd for sure become food for the animals and if not that then he wasn't familiar with the landscape so he would most likely be lost till morning. Neither option sounded pleasant. He pushed his glasses up his nose to secure their place, dug his hand into his pocket, pulled out a wet wipe, cleaned off the ladder as much as possible, and made his way up the tower towards Stella taking each step one by one.

Stella reached the top of the tower. She turned around and held out her hand to Oliver as she helped him up. The sun was now hidden behind the trees in the distance, and the sky slowly faded to night.

"Wow," he said as he stared in awe out in the distance, "this is so cool."

"Yeah. It is," Stella agreed. "And you were going to let fear keep you from experiencing this!"

From the tower, in the not too far distance, they could see perfectly the large screen from the drive-in movie theatre. In front of the screen were a bunch of parked cars, which because of the distance now looked like toy cars awaiting the film. When the night sky arrived in full, The Wizard of Oz began to play. Stella took a seat at the edge of the water tower, her legs dangled off the side while her arms wrapped tight around the railing.

"Too bad there is no sound," Oliver said as he took a seat next to her.

"You need it?"

"Maybe not. This is my mom's favorite movie. Used to watch it all the time. I guess I know the gist of it."

Stella sat up straight. "I know every line by heart," she boasted.

"No, you don't," Oliver said suspiciously.

"Yes, I do."

"Every line?" he questioned. "I don't believe you."

"Challenge accepted!"

The pure joy across Stella's face was enough for him to doubt her again and again. It was clear she liked a playful challenge. Her energy was young, like a school kid determined to win a game of four square because her friends dared her that she couldn't win; Stella was ready for a challenge. This was a moment to shine. She took a deep breath and looked out towards the screen. Sure enough, as the movie began she recited every line perfectly at the exact moment the actors' mouths moved.

Dorothy arrived in Oz clearly not in Kansas anymore. Glinda the good witch made her grand entrance inside her magic bubble; Stella recited the lines, *"Can you help me find my way?" "Then you must go to the Emerald city. Perhaps Oz will help you."* She turned to Oliver and gifted him a confident, 'I told you so,' smile that set his heart aflutter. *"The road to the Emerald City is paved with yellow brick so you cannot miss it." "Come along, Toto."*

The movie continued and Stella hadn't missed a moment. Dorothy came across the Scarecrow and Stella said in her best Scarecrow voice, *"I haven't got a brain, only straw… If your heads were stuffed with straw, like mine, you would probably all live in beautiful places… My life has been so short that I really know nothing whatever. I was only made the day before yesterday… Luckily, when the farmer made my head, one of the first things he did was point my ears so that I heard what was going on… Then he made my nose and my mouth; but I did not speak, because at that time I didn't know what a mouth was for."*

The movie went on and Oliver was mesmerized by what appeared to be Stella's one-woman show. She delivered every word with emotion just like the actors would. The friends on the screen hopped into a carriage in the Land of Oz with a destination of a salon and suddenly Stella stopped reciting the line. A colorful horse appeared on the screen at the same time a longing appeared across her face. "That's my favorite line in the movie," she said. Oliver was having trouble taking his eyes off of her, he was captured by the moment and lost in thought. "What line was that?" he asked. "I missed it."

"The one about the horse being of a different color." She smiled. "There was only one like him in the whole world. He was unique."

Oliver instantly understood why that line meant so much to her because he felt it too. They were both 'different' than what fit the reality of the world they lived in. They too were horses of a different color.

The movie was nearing the end and as the wizard handed out the gifts Stella said in her best impression of The Wizard of Oz, *"You have plenty of courage … all you need is confidence in yourself."* The Tin Man asked, *"How about my heart?"* and she responded, *"Why, as for that, I think you are wrong to want a heart. It makes most people unhappy. If you only knew it, you are in luck not to have a heart."* Then she said, as the Tin Man, *"That must be a matter of opinion … for my part, I will bear all the unhappiness without a murmur, if you will give me a heart."* A hint of pain and hope waved across her eyes. And at that moment Oliver felt the opposite; a tiny piece of his misunderstood, broken heart began to mend. *"Very well, you shall have a heart."*

At the end, when Dorothy finally returned to Kansas, Stella said, *"Oh, Auntie Em! I'm so glad to be home again!"* Stella once again got choked up as her eyes began to water. She continued, *"There is no place like home."* With that the movie ended.

Stella took a moment to compose her emotions. She was a strong woman, no doubt, but that last line struck a chord in her heart. She took another deep breath in and exhaled, successfully calming her emotions, and her tears retreated. She looked over at Oliver who had barely watched the actors on the screen because he was fully captivated by Stella. Watching her recite the lines of this movie was not only impressive it also felt as though the words captured her essence and the way she recited them was the key to the map of who she really was. They both held each other's gaze until she asked, "So, what did you think?"

Oliver sat in the moment a bit longer; then suddenly he began to clap. A slow clap at first and then he began to clap faster and faster and louder and louder until he stood up giving her a standing ovation. "Take a bow, really that was … impressive. Holy smokes!"

Stella let out a wave of excitement and relief. "I used to watch this movie every day," she said as she stood and took a couple of playful bows.

"I mean we all have a favorite movie but, wow, you weren't kidding."

"Well, it was my escape."

A serious tone entered the conversation. "Escape?" he asked.

"Yeah." Stella placed her hands on the top of the railing as her fingers slid against the glossy paint. "I was in the foster system growing up. With every new family this movie brought me comfort … hope."

Oliver was not expecting her to say that or anything close to it. He could feel his anxiety rush back to his body; his armpits began to sweat through his shirt, his throat became dry, and he was trying very hard to sort out the many thoughts that were overloading his head. *Gosh, say something!* he thought. *Man, say something, don't just stand there sweating like a pig and being weird and stuff.* He didn't know what would be the right words to say in that situation. *Are there right words for a situation like this?* he thought. Before he made a total fool out of himself his voice took over with a mind of its own and thank God it did. "I'm sorry to hear that," he found himself saying.

She gave him a sincere, collected smile. "Don't be." And suddenly, led by her calm approach, his anxiety started to die down once again. She continued, "I believe we all have a path, and this happened to be in mine. Besides, there are so many people who had it much harder than me. I turned out just fine."

Oliver believed her. He hesitated to ask this next question, but before he could control his manners his voice was already delivering it. "So do you have a ... a ... family?"

She smiled letting him know it was okay for him to speak freely in front of her and he had permission to ask whatever he wished to know. She continued, "No, I aged out at eighteen. Been on my own ever since, but..." Her eyes began to light up again. "But I have a handsome cat named Simon and the best friend in the whole world. Her name is Julie, and she's got a husband and two very lively kids. They make me feel like I'm a part of their family."

"That's good."

"Yeah. Life's good." This time Stella's smile told a story similar to one a soldier might tell the moment they were told the war was over. One would think that in that instance it wouldn't matter so much if they won or lost; just knowing that they survived the outside battles, survived the internal suffering, survived the loneliness was enough. A smile of strength ... that's what it was. Stella looked up at the stars. "Beautiful night, don't you think?" When Oliver didn't reply, she looked back at him. She caught him in an intense stare as he soaked in every part of her essence. "What?" she said with a giggle.

Still in awe he said, "Nothing," then smiled back at her.

She gave him a playful nudge. "I'm glad you're my adventure buddy."

"Me too." And in that moment, he fell in love with her.

# Adventure Buddies

The next day, Oliver awoke into a wonderful world. He was a man in love, but of course he wasn't going to tell her that. They were adventure buddies, her words, and he didn't want to do or say anything that might result in him losing her friendship. But it was okay because he got to hang out with her all summer long, adventure after adventure.

He still spent much of his free time vacuuming the rug, listening to music, sketching at his desk and existing in his own world, but when Stella was free, she would call him, and off they went on another adventure.

She took him to the bowling alley where she challenged him to a match, best two out of three, and to her surprise he won. Oliver wasn't athletic by any means, but back in high school his parents forced him to join a winter sport, and the bowling team seemed like it required the least amount of athletic ability. Their matches also drew no crowd, which made it even more appealing to Oliver. Never in his life would he have imagined he could impress a girl with his bowling skills, but either Stella was easily impressed or she faked it, though she didn't come off as someone who would ever fake an emotion. She wore them all on her sleeve, released them on impulse and owned every single one of them.

One night a week a local pub did an entire night of live band karaoke. Stella had been sneaking into that bar for years; no one seemed to mind anymore. In fact, one would have assumed that Stella was paid to host the event with the way she approached every patron in the bar and encouraged them to go up and sing a song. She believed in everyone's ability to express themselves; even if their voices were less than wonderful, music was still an important, powerful and fun form of expression, one that everyone could participate in. This gumption was something Oliver admired about her.

"I can't hold a note!" exclaimed a woman in the bar.

Stella shouted over the music, "You don't have to be good! As long as you have fun, that's all that matters... Come on! We will all be here singing with you!" And just like that the woman wrote her name on the karaoke list. Stella sang too, she had a nice voice but her amplified energy on stage was what won the crowd over. Oliver wouldn't dare to sing; he watched from the sidelines but enjoyed every minute of the show.

One of their most memorable outings was when they would go to the park and sit on the stone wall that outlined the creek. They would dangle their feet in the water as the stream flowed gracefully through their toes. And when the evening came, they would venture to Lake Hefner. They would admire the lighthouse as they walked the dirt path to the edge, just in time to catch the sunset. One evening, while they sat at the edge of the lighthouse, Stella professed her love of water. She mentioned she was a Leo, a fire sign, and even though that meant nothing to Oliver, who hardly believed in the signs of the zodiac, she explained to him that the water calmed her flame. It balanced her out. She then asked him what his sign was.

"I don't know," he said.

"What? How can you not know?"

"I just don't."

"When is your birthday?" she asked.

"May eighth."

"Taurus," she said. "Homebody, stubborn, patient, mysterious, a hard worker, quiet until something needs to be said … practical. Yep, it all makes sense." She thought to herself for a moment then asked, "But where does your artistic side come from? We will have to find out your sun and moon sign!" She was getting more excited by the minute. Oliver didn't believe in the hype but couldn't help but smile at the way it made Stella's world light up with flying colors.

"We can definitely be friends," she said, "I love Tauruses."

~  ~  ~

The summer was nearing an end and Stella had invited Oliver to join her at Julie and Kyle's summertime backyard barbeque. The whole neighborhood was invited. The kids ran around playing games and entertaining themselves while the adults socialized and spread some heartfelt gossip while kicking back an ice-cold beer or a hard black cherry lemonade.

Kyle stood over the grill. He wore a clean white apron with a cartoon hot dog embroidered onto the front. Julie stood over his shoulder. She looked down at the hamburgers and hot dogs, which were turning charcoal black. "Are you sure it's not done?"

"Julie, let me do this," Kyle said, a bit irritated.

"I just don't think you're doing it right," she said. Suddenly Stella walked into the backyard, Oliver by her side. This was excellent timing for Kyle; finally Julie would have something else to do other than question his barbequing abilities.

"Hey," Stella said.

"Stella, I'm so glad you made it," Julie said as she leaned in for a hug.

"Of course! I wouldn't miss it." Stella turned and pointed to Oliver. "This is my friend Oliver."

Oliver gave Julie a shy nod. "Pleasure."

In an instant Julie's demeanor changed from a normal woman in her thirties into a young schoolgirl who spoke as though she had read Stella's diary, knew all the secrets and was trying really hard not to spill the beans. "Oliver… It's so nice to finally meet you. I've heard so much about you."

Stella blushed, she leaned over to Julie. "Don't be weird," she whispered.

"Okay." Julie got the message. "Come get a plate. There is plenty of food, have as much as you want. Don't be shy."

Oliver and Stella joined the buffet line with the rest of the guests. They stacked their plates with juicy burgers, hotdogs, pasta salad, fresh watermelon, strawberries, carrots, and potato chips. They grabbed an ice-cold cola from the cooler and then found a place to sit at a picnic table that was painted a fire truck red. Kyle and Julie sat down next to them and the four friends spent the entire day eating, drinking, and getting to know one another. At one point Oliver and Stella played corn hole, a silly yet addictive game where you throw beanbags into a hole across the way. Later on in the evening, and to everyone's surprise, even Oliver's, he participated in a game of tag with the kids. I guess he couldn't resist the cunning charm of the twins asking him to participate.

~  ~  ~

The sun set and the night was dark. Most of the guests were already gone except for a couple neighbors who sat by the bonfire, and their only job was to sober up before making the drive home. Stella and Julie stood in the kitchen talking as they cleaned the dishes. "I like him," Julie said, starting the girl talk.

"I bet you do," Stella replied sharply.

"What's that supposed to mean?"

Stella smiled. "You have him cleaning your living room!"

It was true; the girls had a clear view of Oliver, who stood in the living room, tissue in hand as he dusted the top of the picture frames that hung on the wall.

"Hey, I didn't ask," she defended herself. "I just didn't tell him to stop." The girls laughed. "Besides, I think he enjoys it."

Julie was right; Oliver felt no ill will toward wiping the dust off of the frames. They needed it done, just as much as he needed to do it.

Julie continued, "Anyway, I do like him. I think you two are a good match. I can see it."

"Oh, we're just friends," Stella stated.

Julie shot her a look of disbelief. You didn't need twenty-twenty vision to see that they clearly had something going on. The energy between them was noticeably strong.

"What?" Stella asked. "We are. We don't like each other like that."

"Has he said that to you?" Julie looked certain in her analysis.

Stella thought and innocently replied, "No."

"Have you said that to him?"

"No. But we don't need to. We're friends; that's it."

Stella was sticking to her guns on this one and Julie was exhausted from playing hostess and was not about to fight her on it. Not tonight. She replied, "If you say so."

Oliver entered the kitchen.

"All done?" Julie asked, like a mother would to her child after he claimed his chores were finished.

Oliver let out a chuckle, clearly embarrassed. "Sorry about that. I can't help it. Just a little OCD I guess." He shrugged.

"No need to apologize. Who doesn't appreciate a tidy house? You are welcome anytime."

The three stood in a very brief moment of awkward silence until Stella got a glance at the time from the bird clock that hung above their kitchen table. "We have to take off. Only a couple more days of adventures before school starts up."

"That's right. You must be so excited!" Julie exclaimed.

"Oh yes," Stella said, radiating confidence.

She was going to be attending community college in the fall and was very excited for this. Oliver had placed her news in the depths of his brain a long time ago. He didn't want to think about fall and how Stella's time would then be split between school and work. Would she even have time to be his friend? To go on their legendary adventures? The thoughts were too much to bear, so Oliver buried them.

"You kids have fun," Julie said as she hugged them goodbye.

Julie closed the door. Stella and Oliver walked down the porch steps and continued down the sidewalk. There was not much talking on the walk home. They both knew that their adventures would very soon be put on hold, temporarily of course, and neither one of them wanted to address it.

"Thanks for coming with me," Stella said.

"Thanks for inviting me."

"Did you have fun?"

"Everything's fun with you, Stella."

It was a lovely end to a beautiful summer.

# FALL

# Un Semestre d'Amour

It was officially fall in Oklahoma. The temperature chilled, the air became crisp and the leaves turned beautiful shades of red, orange, and yellow before they danced to the ground and garnished the grass.

As usual Stella woke up with the sun and she and Simon did their morning meditations together. But this day was extra special because today Stella would start a brand-new chapter in her life as an official college student. Unable to contain her excitement she decided to channel her enthusiastic energy into a gratitude meditation. She had a lot to be grateful for and couldn't think of a better way to use that energy. She was certain that life was a circle. When one gave gratitude, they would in turn attract more things to be grateful for.

Stella never really had a plan for her life. She believed that though it was perfectly fine to dream and manifest the life you wanted it was also okay to go with the flow. She trusted that the universe had a timeline all of its own, and no matter what she did the energy belonging to the universe would guide her on the right track, shooting her like a star through the galaxy and on to her next move. All she had to do was show up with a mind and heart that were open to all possibilities. For this very same reason, she wasn't concerned that most people attending her school this semester would be a year or two her junior. You see she had the option to attend college right after high school but passed on the opportunity because when she turned eighteen, she was finally free. Free of the system, free of foster care, free to actually be on her own. She delighted in her sense of freedom and wasn't ready to enter into another institution. At the time she felt strongly that she wouldn't have concentrated or taken college as seriously as she did now.

Months ago, during one of her meditations, she was presented with a thought about embarking on the experience of college. Like those wondrous little surprises in life, something she didn't think she ever wanted became a new adventure that she craved. With a little research she discovered that receiving a college education wasn't as daunting of a task as some people made it out to be and perhaps not totally out of her realm of possibility.

~ ~ ~

Stella arrived at school with her black skirt slightly above her knees, stockings, mini black boots, and a brownish orange blouse, perfect for fall. Her hair was loosely curled and her navy-blue, plaid, checkered backpack rested on her back. The campus was overflowing with eager students. Stella soaked in the energy of excitement as she looked up at the giant red brick building that stood tall in front of her. She couldn't believe she was there. This moment, though a first for her, looked and felt so familiar. A rush of déjà vu flew through her mind's eye, like it did during that wonderful meditation. She glanced down at her class itinerary, which she'd printed earlier that week in anticipation. With a turn of her wrist she caught a glimpse of her watch and rushed off to class.

~  ~  ~

Meanwhile, at the Roads' house, Oliver fell back into his unusual ways. Grace stood outside of their upstairs hallway. She peeked around the door frame to see Oliver in his room, vacuuming that stupid rug again. Jack walked by and noticed a somber look across his wife's face. "What are you looking at?" he asked. Grace was silent. Jack followed suit and peered over his wife's shoulder into Oliver's room.

"He hasn't left this room in weeks," Grace said.

"Where's his girlfriend?"

"He says she's back at school."

"That girl probably decided she didn't want to be friends with him anymore. Decided to use school as an excuse." As the words left Jack's mouth, he immediately realized how awful they sounded. He knew he wasn't going to win a father of the year award anytime soon, but that comment brought him to a new low. He felt it. He also knew that Grace wasn't going to approve of his commentary, nor should she.

She shot him a look of immense disappointment as she scoffed and nudged him out of her way.

"What?" Jack said defensively. But Grace wasn't fooled. He knew what.

~ ~ ~

Weeks seemed to fly by for Stella and she was enjoying every minute of the semester. Aside from her classes she spent most of her spare time in the library. Just being amongst the books made her feel smarter. Simply standing in the library brought a rush of power and potential. Anything she wanted to learn was right there in front of her fingertips. It was a playground for curiosity. She was an excellent student too, never missed a class.

It was a Tuesday and Stella was seated in her French 101 class. The room was very basic, as one would expect from a community college. There was an oversized white board attached to the wall behind the teacher's desk, a map of France on the wall adjacent, the French alphabet bordered on the opposite side of the room and in between the four walls sat twenty-five vintage school desks aligned in perfect rows.

Her professor was a petite lady, straight from Paris, France. She was in her fifties with dark shoulder-length hair, displaying a perfect attitude of sass. As caring as she was towards her students, she somehow managed never to be caught smiling with her teeth. Stella was curious how a woman like her would end up in Northern Oklahoma, the culture was so different. Then again, the same could be asked of herself. Stella laughed at the irony of her thought.

One day, she had asked her professor how she came to be an Oklahoman and received a story that could make a bitter man's heart tear. Her professor, in her perfect French accent, told Stella that she met her husband, Nicholas, when she was at a study abroad program in the States. They fell into a young love, one that they both new would only last that semester. When the semester ended, they said their goodbyes and she went back to Paris. They kept in contact via letters, but with time they lost touch. Then, much to her surprise, on her best friend's wedding day, Nicholas walked through the doors of the church. She couldn't believe it. Apparently, her French girlfriend's husband, a dark and incredibly handsome man from the States, was Nicholas's childhood friend. She could barely contain her excitement. It was such a small world leading to a moment that was certain to be one in a billion. It seemed like fate, so they had no choice but to rekindle their flame, or at least to explore it once more to see if the flame was still simmering.

Thirty days later, they were married and her life forever changed once again when she moved to Oklahoma, United States of America. Though she loved Paris, she loved Nicholas more. They vowed to visit her family and friends twice a year, a promise they managed to keep. "The world we live in is much greater than we know but smaller than we realize," she told Stella. "Remember that."

Stella sat studiously at her desk while she and her classmates listened intently to their professor.

"Aujourd'hui, nous apprenons les verbes... Notez ceci. Today, we are learning verbs... Write this down," she translated.

The students grabbed their pencils and notebooks and began to copy the words written on the board. From the tip of her ear, Stella heard a whispering, "Pst, pst."

She turned to see Landon, a classmate who happened to be extremely handsome. He had short, sandy-blond hair and ocean-blue eyes that were easy to get lost in. His strong jaw and perfect bone structure made all of the girls gush. Stella remembered paging through a book in the library where she came across a picture of a statue that was displayed at the Getty Museum. This stone was sculpted into what was considered the ideal body of a man as perceived by the Ancient Romans; that was Landon.

He looked at her with his mesmerizing eyes and said, "J'aime ton collier."

Stella, who was a little behind on the French translation, looked confused. She wanted to respond but didn't completely understand what he said and was very much caught off guard with him initiating a conversation with her.

Landon noticed her confusion and let out a soft smile. "I love your necklace," he whispered.

Stella placed her hand on her chest as she felt her necklace. It was a rose quartz pendant wrapped in gold wire on a matching chain that rested elegantly on her collarbone. She blushed. "Merci."

"Rose quartz. That's a nice stone," he said.

Stella was shocked and pleasantly surprised that he could point out a rose quartz. Most people just thought it was a pink rock when, in reality, a rose quartz was a stone that carried the spiritual prosperities of love. This stone helped open the heart to all levels of love, including loving oneself. The stone was also said to contain healing prosperities that worked to heal the pieces that were broken, bring the heart harmony, and bring forth true love, unconditional love.

"Pour le coeur," he said, which in English meant "for the heart." "I'm Landon," he said as he held his hand out.

"Stella," she said as their hands met.

"Pleasure to officially meet you," he said while giving her the most intense eye contact she'd ever felt. Stella blushed as she turned back around to face the white board. She couldn't remember what the professor taught that day. The professor's words drowned in the background as Landon took a prominent spot in her thoughts.

~ ~ ~

Stella and Landon fell into young love very quickly. He thought she was adorable and, yes, her views on life were out there, very different from the conservative world he grew up in, but that was one of the things he loved most about her. Not only was she gorgeous but she was also confident and didn't seem to judge him for being a boy and a jock first. She didn't complain when he wanted to hang out with his friends; in fact, she encouraged it, which was different from his past girlfriends.

Stella fell for Landon hard too. Not only was she smitten by his looks and his charm, she felt protected by him. He was a good foot taller than she was and when they went out in public, he always had his arm draped around her shoulder, proud to show everyone that she was his girl, and on top of it all he gave the best hugs. It was always a big bear hug that made Stella feel special.

Stella was such a strong woman, she always had to be, but she had to admit that this time around, it was nice to feel comforted. When she was with him, she was safe. She also loved that they were the same age. Landon had taken a break after high school to help his father on their family farm. He volunteered to work on the farm because he thought that was what his father wanted, a son who followed in his footsteps. One day, his father overheard him explaining to his friends that he really wanted to be in the medical field. His father was steaming mad that Landon would put his own ambition aside to do what he thought he wanted him to do. That day, his father nearly kicked the barn door down and the next day he dragged

Landon down to community college and signed him up. Landon was lucky to have a girl like Stella and a father like the one he had.

Young love is a beautiful thing. Every moment seemed like it belonged in a story book. Stella and Landon hung out with their college friends at the local pub. They enjoyed a beer and live music; laughter was inevitable. Though she wasn't any good at it, Stella loved to play bar darts. "Okay, I'm going for the ten," she would say, "the ten." She would close one eye and align the other perfectly with her target. When she released the dart, it wasn't anywhere near the ten. A bit frustrated, she would shrug it off and take another sip of her beer. "I'll get it next time," she would say.

"I believe you," Landon would respond as he pulled her in for a kiss. He loved her optimism and her competitive nature.

Stella was an unusual kind of competitive, she always said "winning isn't everything, but it sure beats losing so you might as well give it your all and at least try." The playful competition put a little oomph into their dates. One day, they went to the park to throw a football around. "Further, Stella!" he shouted as Stella jogged further into the greenery.

Landon lined up his fingers to the laces of the ball, pulled back his elbow and released. The football darted through the air in a perfect spiral and landed right into Stella's arms. She cradled the ball as she ran towards him.

Her face was like a child's, enjoying every minute of the game. She tried to pass Landon as he gleefully anticipated her every move. He had her cornered and she knew it. If he were to let her get past him on purpose and win the game she would be upset because a move like that, though the gentlemanly thing to do, would make her victory lap falsely achieved so it was better for both of them when he playfully tackled her to the ground. The two laughed together and she gently pushed him off of her. "I want a redo," she said. "I think I figured your plan out this time."

He admired her gumption. "Whatever you want," he said.

Landon was as spontaneous as she was and she loved it. One evening Stella stayed late at the library. She had a biology test the next day and was nowhere near ready for it. As she paged through her notebooks and homemade flash cards, she could feel someone staring at her. She looked up to see Landon sitting at a table across the way, eyes locked in her direction. He knew not to approach her table when she was studying. He was too much of a distraction. Instead they shared flirtatious smiles back and forth across the room until finally Stella mouthed, "Fine." She placed a bookmark in between her pages, closed the book and headed down one of the aisles. Landon gave her a couple seconds then followed her, unable to hide his excitement. He met her in the aisle and the two shared one intense make-out session, one that neither one of them would forget anytime soon.

Then Landon went home and Stella went back to her table to study. The next day, she passed her biology test with flying colors.

# Jack and Grace

Jack pulled up to the driveway of their beautiful home. As he approached the house, he could see Grace through the grand window. She stood in the kitchen preparing dinner as Hannah sat crisscross apple sauce on the island stool, they were both laughing. The sight of their happiness made Jack's heart whole.

He and his wife had been married for nearly thirty-five years. They met in a math class when they were both enrolled in grad school at MIT. He remembered it clearly; he confidently walked into the classroom, took one look at her and instantly lost all feeling in his legs. She one hundred percent took his breath away that day and had every day since. He was in love with her from the moment she turned him down—twice. She was there to gain an education, not to be distracted by boys; that was her excuse and it worked. Until one day, after a midterm lab, he asked her if she would like to join him for a celebratory drink and, much to his surprise, she said, "Yes."

As they chatted over a single-barrel bourbon on ice, Jack knew how lucky he was to be in her company. She was beauty, brains, and had the purest heart he had ever known. In his eyes she was much better than he was and if he wanted to be with her, he would seriously have to step up a level and fully commit to her; no more childish games, one-night stands, or any of the other habits formed during his bachelor lifestyle. Grace was pure, and she deserved nothing but the best. He vowed to be the one to give her that.

The handsome, athletic guy with the winning smile and the most confidence she'd ever seen in a single individual had asked her out twice that semester. Though she was flattered and impressed by his conviction, each time she turned him down. She had always been attracted to a certain type of guy and she could smell a player from miles away. His name was Jack and he was just that, a player. The second time she turned him down she saw a glimpse of disappointment in his eyes. For a brief moment, she thought that maybe she misjudged him; maybe she mistook his confidence for cockiness and perhaps categorized him a bit too quickly. She expressed this to her girlfriends over a Sunday brunch full of bottomless mimosas and girl talk. They confirmed that she may have been a little harsh.

"Girl, just because you go out with a guy doesn't mean you're stuck with him for life," said her friend Tonya, a lively woman who was enrolled there to work on her PhD. "You think that if you say yes to a date you're saying yes to your entire future, and it's not that serious."

If there was one thing for certain you could always trust Tonya to tell it like it was. She continued, "If a guy wanted to take me out that bad, I'd let him. Hey, tuition is high, and Lord knows if nothing else it'll be a free drink, some good conversation and just being around some testosterone…" Tonya couldn't finish as her girlfriends began to laugh. "What are you all laughing about? 'Cause I said testosterone? Ya'll are childish for real. Yeah, I said testosterone and I meant it. When you put male and female energy together, magic happens, like they bring out a brand-new you." Tonya stopped and noticed the silence protruding from her friends.

"Okay, I get it. I can read a room; but trust me, ladies, flirtatious energy, sensual desire, moments that get your heart rate going a bit without running miles in a gym, those are the moments that can add quality to your life. You feel me?" She looked around at her friends and their lack of enthusiasm. She added, "It also helps speed up your metabolism."

"Does it really speed up your metabolism?" one of the girls asked.

Tonya rolled her eyes. "I don't know if it's been proven but, hell, try shedding some stress and being truly happy for a week. I promise you, you could lose an inch off a tummy. It's all about the balance." She took a sip of her mimosa. "Can I get some more champagne?"

Everything Tonya said was entertaining. She was a captivating speaker and quite honestly the words of wisdom she laid upon them that day made sense.

Tonya was accurate when she implied that Grace wasn't good at dating around. She had this misconstrued idea that a date would turn into marriage, which would eventually turn into losing oneself completely and ending up living a life of bitter unhappiness. Just like her sister who had turned into a wife and mother her senior year in high school. Three kids later, and a distant marriage, she barely saw her sister smile except when she was a couple glasses of Moscato in. Grace tried very hard to live a life that was the exact opposite of her sister's so much that sometimes she came to question if there were some potential roads she had shut down too quickly, something important she might be missing out on.

"Okay," Grace said. "Tonya, I hear you."

"The mimosas must be working then."

"Funny."

"I thought so."

"I hear you and I agree. The next time he asks me out, if there is a next time, I will say yes."

"Cheers girl." Tonya held up her glass. "To testing our own boundaries in order to grow and experience this beautiful thing called life."

"Cheers," the girls said in unison as they clinked their glasses.

~ ~ ~

The students were prepping for midterms and Grace was fully prepared for Jack to ask her out again. A study date, if nothing else, would be the perfect excuse. But he never did. Their interaction was nothing more than a respectful "hello." *Damn,* she thought, *I may have completely misjudged that one.* She contemplated asking him on a date, but at the last minute she chickened out. She had never realized how nerve-racking it was to ask someone out. It took a lot just to build up the courage and then to be rejected twice by the same girl she couldn't wrap her head around it. If Grace would have built up the courage to ask someone out and they rejected her, once would have been enough. But thankfully Jack was a strong believer that the third time was a charm. The day after midterms he walked up to Grace and said, "I don't want to come off aggressive or annoying, and if you say no again I promise I got it. But now that midterms are over and we can relax a bit, would you like to come out with me for a celebratory drink? I feel like we earned it."

Much to his surprise she said, "Yes."

~ ~ ~

The two of them sat in an upper-class bourbon bar outside of Cambridge, Massachusetts. They talked about everything under the sun, their families, ambitions, and embarrassing stories from their younger years. Jack would never forget the way she looked in the candlelight, she was soft and stunning. He knew right away that she was special.

She was surprised by how engaged he was in their conversation and impressed by how much of a gentleman he turned out to be.

That night he walked her home. He made sure to place himself on the street side of the sidewalk. When the wind blew, she crossed her arms to warm up and before she had a chance to shiver, he draped his jacket over her shoulders. When they finally arrived at her doorstep, he gave her a hug, his chin perfectly rested on the top of her head. The embrace lasted a moment or two longer than either anticipated. He then apologized as he blushed. "Sorry, just felt good. I didn't want it to end." Jack gave her a kiss on the cheek and told her, "Goodnight, Grace."

She was left speechless. Jack started to walk down the street; he glanced over his shoulder and gave her one more smile. She was smitten.

~ ~ ~

Years later, after graduation, they got married. Jack took a job in finance and Grace held a top position at an insurance agency. They supported each other in every way and grew together. They had the discussion about having kids once. Jack could see himself being a father but made it very clear that it was only if kids were something she wanted. He was perfectly content with just the two of them. Grace said she didn't see herself having kids and that was it. They never spoke of children again, until one night. Jack sat in bed reading the market section of The

Wall Street Journal when Grace walked in wearing her satin nightgown. She rubbed vanilla lotion into her hands. Jack set his paper down and held up his arm making the perfect spot for her to sneak in. She placed her head on his chest. "What's wrong?" he asked as he ran his fingers through her hair.

"Nothing's wrong," she said.

"Grace, something's on your mind. What's going on?"

"I was just thinking." She paused, unsure of how he was going to react. "I want to expand our family. I want to be a mom." The silence in the room was daunting. When she finally looked up, she saw the biggest smile across his face.

"You're going to be a great mother," he said as he placed a kiss on her lips.

Getting pregnant was a much harder journey than they'd expected. They tried for four years and still no luck. When Grace experienced her second miscarriage, she decided she was done trying. The miscarriages were difficult, they were both emotionally and physically traumatizing; something she wouldn't wish upon anyone. In both experiences Jack had been a lifesaver. He was there for her every step of the way, with no judgments and ready to give her all of the emotional support she could ever need. He respected her wishes to stop trying, and with the irony of life, just when they stopped trying was when she found out she was pregnant once again. Oliver was born nine months later. He was their miracle baby.

Grace enjoyed every minute of maternity leave and when it came time to head back to work, she lasted a week before quitting. She decided she wanted to be a stay-at-home mom, words she never in a million years thought would be coming out of her mouth.

Jack said, "If it makes you happy. I'm on board." He then spent the rest of the night readjusting their finances to support their new normal.

As work pulled Jack into the office earlier and kept him later, he didn't fully take the time to understand what unusual behavior Grace seemed to see in Oliver. It was more manageable for him to determine it a phase. Over the years it became more obvious that Oliver wasn't going to follow in his father's footsteps. No football team, no swim team, no late-night high school parties, no prom date, none of the things that 'normal' kids did. This was a hard pill to swallow. He didn't know how to act around Oliver or how to process his emotions suppressed over the years. With time, distance became his norm. This hurt Grace but she knew that Jack loved Oliver. Plus, she couldn't punish him for not knowing how to handle his emotions, it was a difficult situation for anyone, even she was guilty of having feelings every once in a while. Feelings that no mother should have. But the thing about Jack, sometimes a strength and perhaps also his greatest weakness, was that he channeled his emotions into work and the harder he worked the less time he had to feel them. Not the healthiest way to live but certainly a way.

Two weeks after Oliver's twelfth birthday, Grace found out she was pregnant again. Hannah was a beautiful mistake but God given and therefore the perfect addition to make their family complete. Jack looked forward to coming home and seeing her fluffy personality light up his world just like her mother. And there you had it, the Roads family was complete.

~ ~ ~

Jack walked into the kitchen that night. "Hello," he greeted his wife and daughter.

"Hi honey," Grace said as she took her eyes off of the stove and planted a kiss on his cheek. "How was work?"

"Work was work. What are you cooking?"

"Kielbasa, didn't feel like making anything extravagant tonight."

"Well, it smells delicious." Jacked looked over at Hannah who was seated on top of a stool pushed up to the island in the kitchen. She was playing with her dolls in the dollhouse. "And how was your day?" he asked.

"Good!" Hannah exclaimed as she pointed to the doll house in front of her and beamed with excitement. "I got a dream house for Dolly!"

"Look at that! Very cool," he said.

Suddenly the sound of the vacuum made itself present. The mood became damp. Jack looked over to Grace. "That's the fourth time today," she said. "We need to get him out of this house."

Jack nodded in agreement. "I'm going to fix this. Tomorrow."

"What are you going to do?"

"Just trust me. Tomorrow. You'll see."

"Jack!"

"I've had enough of this. He can't just fall apart because some girl doesn't want to hang out with him anymore." He went up the stairs to change out of his work clothes. And then tomorrow came.

# Tomorrow

It was Saturday morning and Jack woke up early. He went for a run around their neighborhood, made coffee, took a shower, got dressed in a casual sweater and well-fitted blue jeans, drank his coffee as he read the paper, hopped into his car, and drove across town to the Community Center. All before eight a.m.

Fall mornings were always breathtaking. The beauty from the colors of the leaves and the refreshing, crisp cool air made it easy for Jack to wake up early and start the glorious day ahead. Today was no exception; if anything it was even more motivating because Jack was on a mission to make today productive. He walked into the Community Center and was immediately greeted by an elderly African American man, his thin legs held up a hefty gut and his hair was filled with grays that matched his moustache. He wore khaki slacks and a navy-blue polo with the words "Community Center" embroidered in royal purple on the right side of it; his name tag on the other side read: "Evan." "Sir, can I help you?" he asked.

"Jack Roads," he said.

"Evan. Nice to meet you." They partook in a handshake. "What can I do for you?"

"I'm curious about your intramural teams," Jack said, getting straight to the point.

"New in town?"

"About four months."

Evan let out a friendly chuckle. "Well, you came to the right place. Joining a team is an easy way to make some friends."

Jack nodded in agreement.

"So what kind of sport are you interested in?" Evan asked.

"It's not for me. It's actually for my son."

"How old?"

"Nineteen."

"Okay, what kind of an athlete is he?"

Jack shrugged. "You know we're still trying to figure that out," he said as he flashed a facetious smile.

"Well, it's late fall so we have basketball, indoor track, and swimming available."

Jack perked up. "A swim team?"

Evan smiled. "Follow me, I'll show you to the pool, the boys are practicing now."

Evan walked down the fluorescently lit hallways. Jack followed. Plaques that honored the participants lined the walls. As Jack's eyes gazed upon them, he felt a rush of excitement. He noticed a giant case full of ribbons, trophies, team photos and memorabilia that sparked so many memories of his own childhood.

In Jack's youth, he'd played a sport each season—football in the fall, swim team in the winter, and baseball in spring. When summer came around, he spent more time playing outdoors with the neighbor kids and every other week participated in some kind of sports camp. Jack loved sports. They taught a person how to win, how to lose, how to set goals, and how to work hard. They allowed for personal achievement as well as helping one develop the skill sets to work with a team in order to achieve something greater than an individual possibly could. And on top of everything else teammates were like brothers. No matter what beef was created prior to a match, when it was time to perform they always had your back.

Evan stopped in front of a wall that contained a giant window that looked into a twenty-five-meter pool, half the size of an Olympic pool. Inside the pool area were boys in their speedos with goggles, shaved heads and swim caps participating in warm-up laps and stretches. Nostalgia came back to Jack as a smile planted itself across his face.

"Revisiting memories?" Evan asked.

"How did you know?"

"You saw the water and your face lit up."

The boys shared a laugh. Jack said, "I was a swimmer all through high school. Some of the best accomplishments of my life happened on that team."

"It's important for kids to be in a sport. Learn how to work as a team. Learn to lose so they can appreciate what it feels like to win."

"Ain't that the truth," Jack agreed. "And it doesn't hurt to make some lifelong friends."

Though there was no doubt in Jack's mind that he and Evan grew up very differently from each other, he also knew that this conversation was much easier and more fitting than any of the conversations he'd had with Oliver. They seemed to be on the same wavelength and Jack found comfort in knowing that he had now met someone who could speak the same language.

Evan chimed in, "The season just started. This is their second practice. Let me speak to the coach. Maybe your son will take after his old man." He grinned.

Jack hoped so. *Wouldn't that be something?* he thought.

~ ~ ~

That night, during a lovely family dinner, Jack announced to Grace, Hannah, and Oliver that Oliver would be joining the intramural swim team at the community center.

"Swim team? Are you serious?" Oliver asked with a wave of panic.

"Yes," Jack said, "I think a sport will do you good. Keep you in shape, allow you to meet new friends, give yourself some confidence. These are all wins."

He caught Grace rolling her eyes. "What?" he asked. She said nothing.

"Dad, I'm not an athlete," Oliver pleaded.

"You played baseball before."

"I played for two seasons because you made me, and I got to first four times. One of those times I was lucky and the other three were walks because I got hit by the ball."

"Well, maybe that wasn't your sport."

"And swimming is? I don't want to be on the team."

Jack's tone became firm. "Look, it's done. I already talked to the coach. You better work on the excitement because you're on the team."

Oliver's blood was boiling; he'd never despised his dad more than he did in that moment. But his dad was forceful. It took every bone in his body for him to build up the confidence to say, "You can't make me do it. I'm an adult."

Jack raised his voice and he slammed his fist onto the table "Really? Whose roof are you living under?"

Oliver's voice backed down. "But Dad—"

"You're doing it. End of discussion," he shouted sternly.

The room fell silent. No one, not even Jack, thought the conversation would go down like that. Oliver looked over to Grace, hoping she would save him. She gently placed her hand onto his. "It wouldn't hurt to give it a try," she gently whispered, "you may enjoy it."

Oliver felt betrayed. He expected this behavior from his father, but his mother had never been one to pressure him. He abruptly scooted his chair back and angrily stomped up the steps to his room.

The rest of dinner was silent until Hannah spoke up. "Can I have seconds?"

"Please?" Grace said.

"Can I have seconds, please, pretty please?" she asked.

Grace placed a second helping on Hannah's plate.

~ ~ ~

Oliver rushed into his room, overwhelmed with the entire situation. He was a mix of emotions: nervousness, fear, anger, sadness. He didn't know how to handle the emotions. His heart rate continued to rise and the unspeakable thoughts that sprinted through his head a mile a minute were enough to make him feel nauseous. He collapsed onto the bed as he closed his eyes and maneuvered into a fetal position. He used his body weight to gently rock himself back and forth while he concentrated heavily on his breathing.

Surprisingly panic attacks did not happen often in Oliver's world. However, three years ago Jack had surprised Oliver for his birthday with tickets to a music festival. This was a very thoughtful gift, right up Oliver's alley. As excited as he was, he was also a bit nervous about spending the day with his father. The two were having a great time; they almost began to bond until a loud 'boom' spread across the crowd. Oliver collapsed in a full-on panic attack. His heart was racing so fast he was certain he was having a heart attack. The paramedics arrived and what was supposed to be a chill evening became a big unwanted, attention-grabbing spectacle, all over what turned out to be a blown-out speaker. Oliver's doctors presented him with a long list of techniques to overcome this should it happen again. He looked them over a couple of times, but they'd never come in handy again until this day.

Minutes later, Oliver started to feel calmer. His symptoms seemed to settle a bit and he was able to rejoin the present. He opened one eye and saw his posters on the wall of his room. He opened the other eye, relaxed his grip on his legs, rolled onto his back and stretched out across the comforter. After a few deep breaths he looked over at his phone, which sat on his desk. He got up, walked across the room, grabbed his phone and texted Stella: *Hey. It's been a while. How are you?* Then he sat his phone down, hoping she would respond.

~  ~  ~

Stella sat at her small kitchen table piled high with school books, unorganized notes, a cob salad in an open takeout container and a half full mug of coffee once scalding but now room temperature. Her nose was buried in her flash cards as she quizzed herself on psychology terms. Blasts of galactic sound effects intruded her space. "Can you turn that down please?" she asked. "I'm trying to study."

Landon sat in the other room spread across her couch; his hands gripped a video game controller as he pointed it intensely at the television. "Ugh, fine," he said.

Stella rolled her eyes as her phone dinged with a text; much to her surprise it was from Oliver. She read the text as Simon, her cat, hopped up next to Landon and sat on him, presumably ready to reclaim his spot on the couch. Stunned by the cat's actions, Landon pushed him off of his chest and onto the floor. Simon turned to Landon, hissed and then ran away.

Landon glanced over at Stella who held up her phone with a grin across her face. "I thought you were studying," he said as he set the controller down and walked over to her. "That means no phones," he said as he playfully tried to take the phone away from her. He started to tickle her sides. Stella laughed. "Who is it anyway?" he said with a flirtatious tone. "Come on, who is it?" He tickled her again and the more she giggled the more he did too.

Stella managed to break away. "It's my friend Oliver," she said. "I need to text him back." For a moment a look of apprehension fell across Landon's face. He quickly recovered before she noticed. He made his way back to the couch, un-paused his game and continued to play, this time with the sound muted.

~ ~ ~

Oliver was filled with jitters making it impossible to sit still. He casually paced back and forth in his room sneaking a peek at his phone every minute or two. Suddenly his phone dinged with a text from Stella. The text read, *Hey! I'm good. Swamped with work and school. It's been too long.* Oliver smiled at this text. He paused for a moment as he thought hard about what to say next. He began to type, then changed his mind and backspaced, then typed again, then backspaced once more. He paused for a moment, took a deep breath, and, as his head began to declutter, he typed, *I miss you. Can we hang out? Maybe you're free on Saturday?* He pressed send and immediately threw his phone on his bed wishing he could undo what he just wrote. Seconds went by that felt like days. His phone dinged. Stella replied, *Let's do coffee a week from this Saturday. I'm booked up until then.* Oliver eyes expanded. That was easier than he'd thought.

Stella looked over at Landon, playing his video game in the other room. Her phone dinged. She read his message, which read, *Okay.* She then set her phone back down as Simon hopped onto the table. He purred as he rubbed his head on her shoulder then made his way towards her gigantic stack of books, the perfect item for him to rub his face against. He looked back at Stella with his majestic green eyes. "My baby," she said as she stroked his silk coat from head to tail. Simon's purr grew louder.

With his still eyes glued to the screen Landon enquired, "Who is this Oliver anyway?"

Stella simply said, "A friend."

"I've never heard you mention him before."

"We haven't seen each other in a while actually. Life just got busy I guess. Don't worry; you have nothing to worry about. We are just friends," Stella assured him.

Landon paused his game and looked over to her. He released a confident chuckle. "Babe, please, look at me. Not many are a competition."

Stella playfully rolled her eyes. He wasn't wrong. That was for sure.

# Long-Lost Friendship

**E**ach day Oliver drew an "x" through a box on his generic calendar that hung from his wall. He was counting down the days until he would be able to see Stella. Just when he thought two weeks couldn't have gone by any slower, the day arrived.

~ ~ ~

Landon awoke alone and shirtless in Stella's bed. He grabbed his shirt and walked into her living room. It was no surprise to him that Stella and Simon were in the middle of a morning meditation. This happened every morning and, though he didn't quite understand it, she claimed it made her feel amazing, alert and alive so he was on board, though he still couldn't wrap his head around how unusual that cat was.

Normally he would never interrupt her practice, but today he needed to go. He had promised his mother that he would help with some yard work. "I'm headed out," he said.

Stella replied without opening her eyes, "I'm cleansing my energy right now."

"Okay… See you later today?"

"Nope. I'm meeting up with my friend Oliver, remember?"

How could he forget? He didn't. He'd been dreading this day since he first heard about it. "Oh yeah. I forgot," he lied. "Well, when are you going to be back?"

She calmly said, "Not sure. We have a lot of catching up to do."

It was a good thing Stella's eyes were closed because Landon shook his head in irritation.

"Don't be jealous," she said.

"I'm not," he lied again.

"Yes you are. I can sense your energy."

Landon rolled his eyes. It annoyed him that he felt some sort of way about her hanging out with this dude and the fact that he was somehow unable to hide his emotions from Stella, even though she sat way across the room with her legs crossed and eyes closed. "Just call me when you're finished."

"I will," she said, and she meant it.

~ ~ ~

Oliver stood in front of the bathroom mirror. This time he wasn't in his normal jeans and a T-shirt; this time he paired his jeans with a navy-blue sweater over a maroon plaid button-down. He looked sharp. He fixed his hair and readjusted his glasses. Jack walked past the bathroom and noticed Oliver dressed to impress. He stopped. "Where are you going?"

Oliver shyly replied, "Hanging out with Stella."

"Stella? Haven't heard that name in a while."

Unable to look his father in the eye Oliver said, "She was busy with school. But we planned today in advance, so we're meeting up."

"Huh. You're not going to miss the swim meet today, right?"

Oliver looked down. "I won't miss it."

"You better not. The team is counting on you."

Under his breath he whispered once again, "I know."

Jack looked Oliver up and down. He had to admit his son looked sophisticated. Jack knew how important outward appearances were. Dressing the part could get you incredibly far in life, but the real reason people dressed up or took time to look their best was because how one presented themselves was said to be a direct reflection of how they felt on the inside. Or wanted to feel. Oliver's attire screamed confidence; therefore, according to Jack's logic, he should feel powerful and important on the inside too, but, as history would come to support, this wasn't the case. If Oliver had to fake it till he made it that would be okay with Jack. At least his son was putting in an effort to step out of his norm and feel better. This was progress; Jack was proud. "Come here," he said.

Oliver looked at his father, unable to move.

"Come on," Jack said as he walked down the hall.

Jack led Oliver into his bathroom. He pulled out a bottle of his finest cologne and handed it to him. "If you're going to look like a million bucks you ought to smell like a million bucks. Remember, confidence is key." Then Jack left the room. Oliver stood there bewildered. Then he applied a dab of cologne to each wrist and another on the left-hand side of his neck.

~ ~ ~

Oliver waited patiently for Stella outside of the coffee shop. The vibrant fall leaves lying on the sidewalk crunched as he paced back and forth. He glanced as his wrist watch; she was late, but he didn't worry. He was certain she would be there.

Just as he pulled out his phone to text her, she came running from afar. "Oliver!" she shouted. "Oliver!"

"Stella!" he shouted back. He was so excited to see her smiling face come rushing towards him he could barely breathe. Stella didn't slow down; instead, she ran full force towards him and leapt into his arms. Much to his surprise he caught her and playfully swung her around. Oliver didn't even know how it happened. It was perfect, like a scene from a movie. He had to blink a few times to make sure everything was really playing out as he saw it. He had never swung a girl around before, he didn't even know he knew how to do it, it just happened. "I missed you so much," he said.

"I missed you too," she replied.

He set her down, slightly embarrassed that he said that out loud.

"You smell good," she said as she smiled in delight.

Oliver blushed. "Thanks." That smile was captivating. It was a ray of sunshine, always lighting up the world around her. Just as he remembered. He knew he missed her but didn't comprehend how much until she was there again staring up at him, radiating joy.

"So, tell me what you've been up to. We have so much to catch up on."

"You first," he insisted.

"Okay, I'll go second, coffee first."

Oliver and Stella grabbed their coffees, a pumpkin latte for Stella and a black coffee with a dash of cream for Oliver. Stella was in the middle of one of her epic stories, a perk of working in the hospitality industry. "So, I'm standing there, and this lady is trying to return this cooking pan, which she'd clearly used. There is still food dried to the bottom of this pan. But she will not back down. So, I get my manager and guess what…"

Oliver took a moment to respond, he was enthralled by her passion. "You took it back?" he guessed.

"We took it back. Full refund! Isn't that some bunny turds?"

Oliver laughed. "Bunny turds. Yes."

"And Julie and the kids were right there to witness it." Stella went on and on. She could talk for hours on end. Oliver didn't mind; he actually enjoyed every minute of it. He preferred to listen. He was good at it too.

He looked at his watch. "Oh shit."

"What?"

"I have to go."

Stella looked surprised. "Wait, what? I thought we were hanging out today."

"We just did."

"No, all day. Like we used to."

"I'm sorry. I have a prior commitment," he said. It was painful for him to say it to her because the truth was he didn't ever want this day to end, but he also had to go or he was going to be very, very late to his swim meet.

"I have a prior commitment," she mocked with a kind-hearted spirit. Oliver didn't react, and Stella became serious. "Come on, Oliver, very funny. What are you up too?"

Oliver placed his hands awkwardly into his pockets. "It's nothing," he said as he looked away.

Stella stared him down and placed her hands on her hips. "Oliver? Are you bored with me?" she asked, half joking and half serious. Oliver looked at her directly in her eyes and shook his head no. "Oh my gosh, you are, aren't you?" Stella said in amusement as if she was reciting a line from an overdramatic play.

"Okay, you know what … fine," he said in an irritated tone. "Give me your phone."

Stella handed him her phone. He opened up the memos section, typed in an address and handed it back to her. "I really do have to go. Meet me at this address in one hour." He took off down the road in an agitated jaunt.

Stella stood speechless on the sidewalk as her curiosity began to brew.

~ ~ ~

Exactly one hour later, she arrived at the address he had given her. She double and triple-checked that the address he had given her matched the address on the facade of the building in front of her. He had brought her to the community center? Confused would be an understatement.

Stella cautiously entered the building where she was greeted by a nice gentleman named Evan. "You look lost," he said with a friendly smile.

"I don't know exactly why I'm here. A friend told me to meet him here at three."

"You must be here for the swim meet," he said.

"Swim meet?"

"It's the only thing we've got going on today." Evan pointed to the left. "It's down this hallway and then take the second right; you'll run into the pool. I would take you myself, but I've got to watch the door."

Stella became more intrigued by the minute. She politely thanked Evan and followed his instructions down the hallway.

She made the second right and was greeted by a giant window with a perfect view of the pool area. As she peeked through the window, her jaw dropped as she saw athletes in their swim gear partaking in stretches and warm-ups preparing for their meet. Stella's eyes grew wide with surprise as a group of athletes started to disperse and there, standing amongst them, was Oliver in a speedo. His goggles were wrapped around his wrist, the details of the race tattooed on his thigh with a black permanent marker and a navy-blue swim cap was filled with white powder and ready to cover up his luxurious head of hair. Oliver could sense a stare; he turned his head and their eyes met. Stella stood frozen. Never in a million years would she have seen this coming. She didn't know how to react. Everything about this moment felt completely out of character. Oliver instantly regretted inviting her. This encounter was easily a billion times more awkward then he could have imagined. With every ounce of courage he had left in him he raised his hand and gave her a flimsy wave.

Stella, a half a second behind as her brain needed time to catch up with her eyes, let out a nervous laugh, which she caught immediately and covered her mouth in embarrassment. She then waved back at him, beaming.

She took a seat on the bleachers and like clockwork the announcer came over the PA system. "We are going into heat four, medley relay."

Now, it was just a couple weeks ago that Oliver had learned what exactly a medley relay was. It was a race in which each member of the team completed one of the four strokes. This was Oliver's first.

"In lane seven," the announcer continued, "we have a new member, Oliver Roads; he is participating in his first medley relay of the season, performing breast stroke for his teammates."

One teammate from each team hopped into the water, turned away from the lane and placed their feet on the wall of the pool.

"Swimmers, take your mark," the announcer said.

At that moment they each held on to the base of the block that hovered over each lane of the pool and hoisted themselves up so their upper bodies were held partially above the water's surface.

"Get set," he said. And as the blow horn sounded the swimmers pushed off of the wall, gliding like seals through the water backstroking down the lane.

The other three members stood in a line behind them cheering on their teammates while anxiously awaiting their turn.

It was almost Oliver's turn. He took his eyes away from Stella, placed his goggles over his eyes and pushed them tightly against his face, triple-checking that they were secure; the last thing he wanted was for water to leak in. He took his mark on the block and, as the previous swimmers reached behind and touched the wall, he dove over his teammate's head and into the pool. Remembering what his coach advised, he glided underneath the water as far as he could. He had to admit that he enjoyed being under the water. When his head was submerged, it drowned out the outside noise and his world became quiet. But then his lungs would run out of the air that they craved and he would emerge on the surface and be back to his reality.

He began to swim the breaststroke. His arms moved straight in front for a split second then swooped around into a prayer-like position and back out once again while his legs kicked out and around like a frog's and his head bobbed in and out of the water simultaneously. This stroke was naturally the slowest paced one of the medleys, perfect for Oliver.

Impressed by the event, Stella cheered loudly from the bleachers, so much that Jack and Grace, in unison, glanced over in her direction and shared the same thought. *Could that be the mythological Stella?* Hannah was preoccupied as she consumed her bowl of SpaghettiOs.

Even though Oliver swam his heart out and his team had given him a hefty lead he was still much slower than the other swimmers who were quick to catch up and surpass him. He reached the wall and the third swimmer from his team flew off the block, dove into the water, and swam a butterfly stroke.

Stella continued to cheer as Oliver hopped out of the pool and turned to watch his team complete the race. Much to Oliver's surprise his hands clapped together in excitement. He hated to admit it but the race was kind of exciting.

The third swimmer on their team attempted to close the gap, but they had fallen too far behind. By the time he reached the wall the fourth swimmer dove off the block and freestyled as fast as he could down the pool.

The swimmer was fast but not fast enough. As he reached the edge of the pool the team immediately turned toward the giant aquatic scoreboard displayed on the wall. The final times for each lane as well as their placement were posted within seconds. Oliver's team landed in sixth place out of eight. The entire team dropped their head in disappointment except for Oliver who was completely exhausted and out of breath but beaming with joy as he turned to the crowd and saw Stella wave her hands in the air and continue to cheer.

~ ~ ~

Oliver emerged from the locker room in his everyday clothes. He greeted his family in the lobby where his mom gave him a giant hug and raved about how proud she was of him. Oliver was expecting his father to do the exact opposite; sixth place wasn't great and he knew it. But much to his surprise Jack placed his hand on his shoulder and said, "Sixth place isn't last. Now we've got room to improve. You did good; next time I'm sure you'll do great."

Oliver let out a sigh of relief. He was pleasantly surprised, the events of the day kind of made him feel … good.

He informed his parents that he was going to hang out with the teammates. This was a lie but one his parents would buy. Jack smiled in complete support. He was so thrilled to hear this that he forgot to ask his son if it was Stella who they saw cheering loudly in the crowd.

Oliver walked up to Stella. Her jaw dropped open in disbelief. "I can't believe you joined a swim team. I'm shocked."

"My dad made me and clearly I'm not good at it."

"I thought you were great! Look, you got a ribbon," she said as she pointed to the purple ribbon in his hand that read, "Participant."

"It's intramurals," he said, "everyone gets a ribbon."

"Still, you earned it. The real shock is that you managed to keep this all a secret. Why would you not tell me? This is an adventure, Mr. Twist!"

Oliver threw his head back in distress. "Can we please stop talking about this? I'm just glad it's over."

"Fine. Changing the subject. What do you want to do?" she asked.

"I'm not sure. Just relax I guess, let loose, have a good time."

"I know just the place."

~ ~ ~

Stella and Oliver continued their Saturday at the bowling alley. It brought back so many memories from their summer adventures. Bowling ball in hand, Stella set up her stroke. She lined her feet up on the arrows and focused on the pins ahead. As she walked forward her arm swung back; before she could finish the stroke Oliver had crept up behind her and snatched the ball right out of her hands. She laughed and playfully turned around to get him back. She caught him in the corner where he easily surrendered and handed her back the ball.

Stella noticed that there was something about Oliver that was different than before. He seemed to be more ...*confident? Happy? Flirtatious? Nope, confident,* she concluded. *Confident and happy.* Either way, she liked it, a lot.

Their game consisted of a series of strikes, spares and dramatic splits. It was the tenth frame and they were a couple points from each other, Stella in the lead. Oliver was the last to bowl; his first ball split the pins and his second ball would determine the winner. "No funny business," he said as he grabbed his blue marbled bowling ball. "I mean it."

"Who me? Never," she joked.

Oliver lined up his feet on the arrows. He took a deep breath and with perfect form took three steps towards the lane. He released the ball with the perfect amount of speed and spin. The ball rolled down the lane and knocked over one of the two split pins. That pin slid across the way and knocked the final pin to the floor. A perfect spare and enough to win him the game. Oliver jumped up in the air. He walked back to Stella who was waiting for him ready for a high five like a supportive loser.

"Good game," she said.

"You see that?" he said. "Bowling is much more my speed. Though you've obviously been practicing since the last time we played."

She smiled, "Thanks for noticing."

He took a seat next to her. "I missed hanging out with you."

"Me too." And she meant it.

"Just like old times."

They shared a smile. "So, what's next?" she asked.

"Oh, you have more time?" he asked, a bit surprised.

"Of course I do! All day, remember?"

"It's six in the evening; I would say the day is long gone."

"Are you trying to get rid of me again?"

"Never. You hungry?"

"I could definitely eat."

The two returned their bowling shoes and headed to a diner across the street.

~ ~ ~

The diner across the street wasn't busy at that time of day. It had a very simple, home-like ambiance, sun-yellow walls decorated with wooden trinkets and wooden tables. Their giant menu included breakfast all day, which was perfect because the swim meet had made Oliver hungry and he was in the mood for their French toast.

They ate their meals cheerily as they discussed everything under the sun. Stella's phone lay upside down on top of the table. Every once in a while, it would vibrate and she would turn it over, take a quick glance and, without responding, place it face down once again. The third time this happened Oliver asked, "Do you need to get that?"

"No," she said, but her face said otherwise.

"Are you sure?"

"Yeah. It's just this guy I've been seeing. He knows I'm catching up with you today."

Oliver's heart sunk a bit with the news that she was dating someone. He realized how naive he'd been. Of course a girl like Stella would have a boyfriend, he thought. Besides, she kept referring to him as a friend. All the evidence was there, he just hadn't paid any attention to it. "Boyfriend?" he asked casually.

"Yeah." She smiled. "We met at school and have been seeing each other for a little over a month."

"What's his name?"

"Landon."

Oliver didn't know how to respond, but he definitely couldn't say what he thought, which was, *Landon? Sounds like he'd be a douche.* Then he quickly realized how unfair of a thought that was. People were quick to judge him and that didn't make him feel good; he didn't want to be one to return the unwanted gesture.

Stella spoke, bringing him back to reality. "What about you? Are you seeing anyone?"

"No."

Stella's phone vibrated against the table once again. "You sure you don't have to take that?"

Stella stared at her phone. She hesitated. "Yeah. It's fine."

He could tell that the words coming out of her mouth didn't match the inner turmoil. "Do you love him?" he heard himself ask and immediately wished he hadn't.

A sparkle twinkled in her eye. "I've said it to him before. I told him I love him. But I love everyone." She laughed nervously.

Oliver laughed too, he knew that about Stella. It was a word she used lightly because she truly loved everything and everyone.

"It kind of just came out," she said. "He's never really said it back, which is fine." A hint of sadness appeared over her face.

"That doesn't mean he doesn't love you," Oliver said, bringing her out of her wandering thoughts and back to the conversation.

"Hmm?"

"Yeah, I mean people don't have to say, 'I love you,' to show that they love someone. Sometimes it's the, 'Text me when you get home,' or 'Drive safe,' or 'It's cold, take my jacket.' Things like that… They all translate to, 'I love you.' All of them."

Stella looked up at Oliver in awe. That was the second time that night that she'd seen a new side of him.

He noticed her stare. "What?" he asked.

"I'm speechless. All this wisdom from the man who said he doesn't know if love exists."

Oliver smiled shyly. They shared a simple, yet beautiful moment until her phone vibrated again. This time she turned it over and read a text from Landon that read, *Come home. I miss you.*

"I should probably go," she said as she gathered her belongings from the booth. "Hey, are you free Friday?"

"Oomph, I'll have to check my very busy schedule," he said with an overload of sarcasm. "Yes, I'm always free."

"Some of my friends from school are having a pumpkin party. Do you want to come?"

"A pumpkin party?"

"Yeah, you know; carve a pumpkin, have a beer—" she caught herself "—or a club soda."

Oliver smiled. Though a party with people did not seem like a fun way to spend a Friday night, he would do anything to spend more time with Stella. "I'll be there."

"Okay, I'm so excited! I'll text you the details. Oh, costumes are mandatory."

Stella walked away in her signature walk with a pep to her step. Oliver turned pale as the words "costume" and "mandatory" flashed in his cranium.

# The Pumpkin Party

Oliver stood on the doorstep of a modest and rustic red brick home. The lawn was a tad overgrown, and the paint on the white picket fence was worn and beginning to chip away. There were two lounge beach chairs sitting in the front lawn and half of the roof and some windows were lined with cheap holiday lights left over from the previous Christmas.

There were a couple tacky-looking Halloween decorations in the front as well, a few skeleton bones in the grass, a jack-o'-lantern flag in the flag holder and a black spider attached to the front foyer that would drop every time it sensed movement and then 'climb' back up into its web. It was clear to Oliver and the rest of the neighborhood that this house was occupied by college students.

He rang the doorbell. He stood there nervous, constantly reminding himself that he was indeed invited and, even though this wasn't something that sounded fun, he was there because Stella had asked him to come. And that was enough of a reason.

He stood there for what felt like hours before the bright red door opened and a very attractive girl with long copper hair and bold, brown eyes opened the door. The girl, who was dressed as a red fox but aside from the ears and tail looked more like a lingerie model, stood at the door. She looked at Oliver as though he was lost. "Can I help you?" she asked.

Oliver took a second to respond, he was feeling a bit out of place. When he finally found his words he said, "I'm Oliver. Stella's friend."

"Oh, yeah," she said, raising her voice an octave. That and her forced enthusiasm made her sound much friendlier than before.

Oliver could hear Stella's voice from inside shout, "Holly, who is it?" Stella appeared over Holly's shoulder. "Hi!" she said. "Nice costume!" Then she looked him up and down. "What are you?" she asked.

Stella was dressed as a deer, in a costume just as risqué as Holly's. Apparently this was the college version of Halloween and Oliver didn't get the memo. He was dressed in a full tuxedo with a name tag that read, "Apology." Stella read the name tag. "Apology?" she questioned.

Oliver blushed. "Oh, I'm a formal apology," he said as he gestured to his tuxedo.

Holly let out a roar of laughter. "Formal apology, I get it! Funny." She then opened the door further and gestured for him to enter. "Come on in!"

Oliver followed Stella and Holly into the house. "The bathroom's over there if you need it," Holly said, gesturing down a long hallway, "other than that, the party's in here." They walked into the kitchen, which had a tiny living room area attached. "Help yourself to whatever you want and have fun!" She went over to a group of friends in the corner.

The kitchen counters were piled high with bottles of cheap vodka, tequila, some mixers and plastic cups. There was also beer, lots of beer. Chips, cookies, a cheese and meat board, popcorn, caramel apples and holiday-themed treats filled the kitchen table. The furniture in the living room was pushed to the wall leaving a giant open space lined with newspapers. The room was filled with young college students. Stella guided Oliver to a group of guys who stood in a circle over by the libations. She tapped one of them on the shoulder. Oliver didn't even have to wait for him to turn around and introduce himself; he knew exactly who he was. He saw that this guy was dressed as a hunter; a deer and a hunter— he immediately put two and two together. *The perfect couple's costume, overdone but a solid choice,* he thought.

"Landon, this is my good friend, Oliver," Stella said with a smile on her face.

Landon looked him up and down. "Oliver ... interesting name."

There was an awkward silence as Oliver didn't know exactly how to respond to that, not really a question and not particularly an inviting statement. Suddenly he heard himself say, "Landon... I like yours too."

Landon let out a slight chuckle. He puffed his chest up, far from a subtle move, as he placed his arm around Stella and pulled her close. "Nice to finally meet you. My girlfriend has told me so much about you."

Stella forced a smile. She could feel the tension, it was hard to miss, and she didn't like it.

Suddenly Holly stood up on a chair; she shouted to her friends, "Everyone, can I have your attention please?"

Everyone stopped talking and stared up at her. All eyes were on her and she enjoyed every minute of it but pretended that she didn't. She swayed slightly upon the chair but managed to regain her balance without losing a drop of alcohol from her red solo cup. She adjusted her voice again as she forced it up an octave. "Welcome to my pumpkin party! I'm so glad you could all make it. Love the costumes! You all look so cute! Selfie!" she cheered as she took out her phone and snapped a picture. "Awesome, we all look so good! Okay, now back to the festivities! Grab a newspaper and a drink and let's carve these pumpkins!" she hopped off of the chair. "Oh yeah," she shouted, "make sure you keep all the pumpkin guts on the newspaper or you're staying after to clean up! I'm serious."

The entire party grabbed a pumpkin from a pile in the back yard and a carving knife. They spaced out on the newspaper that lined the living room floor and began to carve their pumpkins. Stella sat in between Oliver and Landon. She knew that she was the only one Oliver knew at the party and therefore may have spent more of her time talking in his direction.

"What are you going to carve?" she asked Oliver.

"It's a secret," he said.

"You're really not going to tell me?"

"Nope, what are you going to carve?"

"It's a secret," she mocked.

"Guess we will both be surprised then," he said, unwilling to budge.

Stella let out a playful giggle. "Guess so."

Landon was busy enjoying the company of his other friends but the constant giggling between Oliver and Stella didn't go unnoticed. It was borderline flirtatious and not okay with him. When he finished his carving early, he told Stella that he was going to hang out with his buddies around the campfire. She said that she and Oliver would join them later when they were finished. He planted a kiss on her lips and exited into the yard.

~ ~ ~

The sun went down, and Oliver and Stella were the last to finish their pumpkins. They grabbed a candle from the counter and walked out of the house and into the back yard. They were greeted by a walkway lined with carved pumpkins each glowing wonderfully in the dark night under the full moon. Stella made her way to the end of the line, bent down on her knees and placed her lit pumpkin on the sidewalk; it was beautifully carved with seashells on the base of a wave.

"Seashells," Oliver observed.

"Yes. Simply because they are beautiful."

"And you love the water," he remembered.

"That too. So, let's see what you made."

Oliver bent down next to her and placed his lit up pumpkin next to hers. Her jaw dropped in awe as she stared at his carved pumpkin, which let out a glow of emerald green. "Oh my gosh."

Oliver smiled; his pumpkin had turned out exactly as he had hoped it would. He managed to carve a masterpiece from her favorite work of art.

"The Emerald City," she said breathlessly. "It's beautiful... How did you get it to glow green?"

"I borrowed the green filter from the Christmas lights in the window. Didn't think Holly would mind."

Stella shook her head in wonder. "Wow... impressive."

After a few moments Oliver brought Stella back to reality when he asked, "Where's Landon?"

She looked around. "By the fire I think. I'm not worried." She shivered ever so slightly. Oliver saw this and quickly took off his jacket and placed it over her shoulders.

"Maybe we should go by the fire too?" he suggested.

Most of the guests were outside laughing by the bright burning flames in the fire pit. Stella and Oliver made their way across the yard to join the party. As they approached, two people moved away from the crowd, revealing a young, intoxicated girl sitting in Landon's lap. His arms were around her in a small cuddle and their faces were very close to making out. Landon felt a sensation of someone's stare; he looked up to see Stella's intense glare. He quickly turned pale as he saw her eyes shift from a look of disgust to eyes that were filling rapidly with tears. She immediately ran towards the house. Landon threw the girl off of him and ran after her. "Stella, wait. Stella!"

Unsure of how to react, Oliver stood by the fire like a deer in headlights as the whole party looked his way. He was secretly hoping that Holly would jump up and know what to do, but she was trashed, passed out with her face in a pizza box. Beyond uncomfortable, Oliver turned away from the wandering eyes and powerwalked towards the house.

Landon finally caught up to Stella in the front of the yard. She was furious. He gently reached out, grabbed her arm and swung her around. "Stella, wait. It's not what it looks like," he pleaded.

"Really? On top of what I just saw you're also going to lie to me?"

"I'm not lying. We were just talking."

Stella's emotions were running high, but she did her best to contain them. "You want to change your answer?" she asked. "I'll give you five seconds to tell me the truth."

"Don't be like that."

"Five … four…"

"Stop. Okay baby, nothing happened."

Stella didn't realize how great of a liar he was. "Three … two…"

"What do you want me to do? Say I'm sorry?"

"That's a start."

A rage over took Landon; he snapped. "Fine! I'm sorry you saw us talking; I'm sorry you brought that weirdo to this party; I'm sorry you embarrassed the both of us in front of our friends!"

Hostility filled the air between them. Stella was fuming; her heart was breaking, not only by his actions but also because of his hurtful words about Oliver. "One," she said calmly yet sternly. "Come on, Oliver."

She walked away with her arms crossed tightly against her chest. Landon turned to see Oliver, silent and reserved, behind him. Oliver began to follow Stella. To avoid confrontation, he passed Landon with his head tilted down and his eyes glued to the ground, certain not to make eye contact, a guy like Landon could probably smell his fear. Landon waited till Oliver passed him then took a giant step towards his path and gave him an aggressive push from behind. Much to Landon's surprise and Oliver's, Oliver said, "Don't push me, man," as he shoved him back with all of his might. Landon stumbled to the ground. Oliver picked up his pace and ran after Stella.

Landon stood back up. "Guys like you don't win, man!" he shouted as he watched them go. He then retreated back to the party.

Thank goodness the semester was almost over. Landon and Stella didn't exchange one word the rest of the semester. Aside from some curious glances here and there they avoided each other. It was awkward but life went on.

# WINTER

# The Tree Topper

Winter came and the Roads house perfectly captured the spirit of Christmas. It was as if their decorations were hand-picked by the set designer of a holiday movie. Mrs. Roads was most proud of her collection of vintage Christmas houses, an heirloom passed down from her grandmother. The outside of their home was breathtaking too. The snow-covered lawn was occupied by three gold-lit reindeer and a matching display of the Christmas Nativity Scene. Gold icicles twinkled as they outlined the roof of the house and a beautiful garland piece with glittering gold lights and a maroon ribbon lined each window.

The spirit of Christmas was very much present inside of their home as well. Grace had spent a full two days unloading box after box of Christmas decorations from their basement. Christmas was her favorite time of year. She remembered all of the fun holiday traditions her family had, such as baking cut-out cookies, attending church on Christmas Eve, and her favorite tradition of all, decorating the tree. When she went off to college, she never expected to be married or have a family of her own. She saw herself as a career woman with no time for anything else. With a mentality of two priorities—study and work—her love of decorating for the holiday had simmered and eventually vanished. It was easier to pay someone else to set up the decorations, yet some years' time flew by so quickly she completely forgot to hire someone and therefore went without. It wasn't until Oliver was born that she regained the desire to revive and lead the family traditions that she had cherished long ago.

Grace, Jack, Oliver and Hannah admired their beautifully decorated Christmas tree. The colored lights shone through the branches of the evergreen making the glitter on the fun-colored ornaments twinkle. This tree resembled the one Oliver had when he was a kid, but when he had gotten older and lost interest his mother had decided to decorate the tree with her own tastes, golden lights and ornaments with accents of red bows. A classical and charming Christmas aesthetic. But once Hannah was born Grace changed back to the fun, kid friendly colored lights and ornaments that looked to her like knickknacks. It may not have matched the rest of her décor, but it made Hannah happy. A small price to pay to see Hannah's face light up at the display of colors, just as Oliver's once did. The one thing she would not cave in on was the tree topper. Years ago, she had inherited a tree topper from her grandmother. It was a beautifully stunning white and gold angel and that tree topper wasn't going anywhere.

Jack pulled out the precious angel from the box and handed it to Oliver. "Son, would you like to do the honors?"

A little stunned, Oliver smiled as he gently took the angel from his father's hands. Hannah ran up to him and beamed at the angel. "She's so pretty!"

Without a moment's hesitation he said, "How about you put it on top?"

Hannah's face lit up with joy. Than it dawned on her. "But I can't reach."

Oliver handed her the angel. He walked up beside her and put his arm around her waist. "On three, jump," he said. "Ready?"

She nodded.

"One, two, three." Hannah jumped as Oliver lifted her up to the top of the tree. Jack and Grace watched with humbled happiness, this already felt like it was going to be a very merry Christmas.

Once the angel was placed nicely on the top of the tree, Hannah's feet landed gracefully back on the floor. Suddenly a phone dinged. "What was that?" Jack asked, looking curiously around the room.

"My alarm," Oliver said, "I've got to go." He quickly grabbed his phone, which lay on the coffee table, and headed towards the coat rack conveniently stationed next to the front door.

"Where are you going?" Grace asked, bewildered.

Oliver grabbed his coat. He put an arm in one sleeve, swung it over his shoulder and slid his other arm inside.

He answered his mother casually. "Stella and I are going to the store to participate in the gifts of gratitude thing."

"What is the gifts of gratitude?" Jack asked.

"It's a program where underprivileged kids write down a present that they want for Christmas," Oliver explained, "then people go to the store, buy it and wrap it up, and then on Christmas Day Santa delivers it to them."

"That's so sweet." Grace beamed with pride as she placed her hand over her heart.

"It's Stella's idea," he gushed. "Every year, she got a present from them growing up so now it's become a tradition of hers to give back." Stella had such a good heart, pure. He loved that about her. No matter the rough patches she may have endured she had never let the cruelty of the world effect the actions of her heart. She always held her head high and was the first to help another.

"I want to go!" Hannah jumped up and down with excitement. "Olly, can I go?"

"Sweetheart," Jack said kindly, "I think your brother and Stella want to do this by themselves."

Oliver appreciated Jack chiming in. He had told his mom that he and Stella were kind of, sort of going out. It was a very weird and uncomfortable conversation that he quickly stashed away from his memory. He didn't want to tell her, she kind of pressed. Plus, since he had never really had a girlfriend before, he didn't know if that was something you told your parents or not. Of course, he knew that she would tell his father, they didn't keep secrets from each other, ever. But much to his surprise Jack never brought it up to him. It wasn't like his dad to refrain from commentary.

"No, but I really, really want to go!" Hannah grew loud. "Please, Olly. Please?" she begged.

Oliver took a look at his sister who was bouncing up and down like she had ants in her pants. Her big eyes of wonder stared up at him. How could he say no? "Go get your coat," he said.

Hannah cheered as she ran over to the door and put on her pink fluffy winter coat.

"Do you need some money?" Grace asked.

"No. Thanks though," Oliver replied as he grabbed the car keys.

Oliver and Hannah exited the house. Jack waited for the front door to shut completely then looked over to Grace. "Looks like our kids are the happiest we've ever seen them. Both of them," he gloated, "and you were worried about making the move."

Grace smiled in his direction. "Very happy," she agreed. She placed her finger on the top of his chest and with a seductive smile began to trace it down his body. "So, here we are, all alone. Just the two of us. What do we do now?"

"I can think of a few things," Jack said as he grabbed her hand, gave her a twirl, pulled her in close, and, when she least expected it, dipped her. Soft, playful laughter erupted from her core and radiated from her smile. Jack leaned down and gave her a passionate kiss on her lips.

Yes, this was going to be a very Merry Christmas.

# Gifts of Gratitude

One of the things Oliver loved about Christmas was the fact that the night fell early. It was a little past five and already the sky was dark as could be. The lights beamed from windows of the department store, lighting up a small section of the snowy sidewalk. Oliver and Hannah walked up to the store's entrance where Stella stood in her elegant raspberry-colored woolen pea coat and black gloves with a faux fur trim. Her face lit up at the sight of them. "Hi! Who's this?" she said as she bent down to Hannah's eye level.

Hannah's face lit up. "I'm Hannah!"

Stella, as pleasant and inviting as ever, said, "It's nice to meet you, Hannah! I'm Stella."

Hannah bashfully smiled, she was not one to be nervous, but the angelic presence radiating from Stella had given her a hint of shyness. She glanced up at Oliver then back to Stella. "My daddy didn't think you were real," she said.

Oliver blushed in embarrassment.

Stella was completely fascinated with this conversation. "Oh?" she replied.

Hannah nodded her head up and down. "I'm glad you are."

"Thanks, me too," she said as she gave Hannah a playful wink. Stella stood back up.

"Sorry," Oliver apologized, "she wanted to tag along, and I couldn't say no."

Stella shrugged it off. "Don't be sorry," she said. "The more the merrier!" She planted a kiss on his lips. Oliver kissed her back.

"Eww," Hannah shrieked.

Oliver and Stella laughed. "Come on, let's go," Hannah said. As she led the way, Stella snuck another kiss.

~ ~ ~

When Stella first met Oliver that night at The Dreslen, she was not really attracted to him. Sure, he was an attractive guy, but never did she think they would eventually call each other boyfriend and girlfriend. They were each so different from the world yet equally as different from one another. She enjoyed being around people, spreading love and gracing the world with her positive perspective. Oliver would rather stay inside; he kept to himself and didn't seem to believe in the perfectly planned path of the universe, or anything for that matter. She was intrigued by him, curious, and by the end of that night she knew that they were two souls living in this world dancing to the rhythm of their own drum. As different as they may have been, in a unique way they were just as similar.

Their summer adventures together were wonderful. At the time she couldn't quite put her finger on why it felt so good to be around him. They had become good friends and she cared for him deeply, but that was always part of the reason why she never saw their friendship moving towards anything more. She enjoyed his company so much; she'd never want to be without it. Friendships could get messy once a line had been crossed. If things didn't work out between the two of them it would break her heart. She was convinced it was better to set the possibility aside altogether.

When fall came, she didn't intentionally drift away from him, it just seemed to happen. When he finally texted her, her heart fluttered a bit. She hadn't felt that in a while. Then later, during their "all day adventure", when they sat at the diner and he explained love to her from a completely different perspective than she'd ever heard before, he managed to open her eyes. It was the words of their conversation and the way he looked at her when she spoke about love that made her realize in that moment that he was speaking about his own actions; the jacket, the text me when you're home, the drive safe. He loved her; he just had an indirect way of expressing it. This realization reopened her mind to the reality of them being a possibility although she suspected that he would never let her know how much he truly cared for her.

The night of the pumpkin party, after the unwanted show between Stella and Landon, her emotions were all over the place. She was hurt and upset, but not with Landon, with herself. She couldn't understand why she had tolerated for so long a love from Landon that was clearly undeserving of hers.

Oliver drove her back to her apartment that night. The car ride was silent. Stella stared out the window, replaying the events of the evening over and over in her mind. Every once in a while, a tear would stream down her cheek; she didn't even flinch. When they arrived at her apartment, Oliver put the car in park. "Home sweet home," he said, trying to lighten the mood. "You going to be okay?" he asked.

Stella turned to him and nodded. She unbuckled her seat belt and reached towards the handle of the car door. Suddenly she turned back to him and asked, "Oliver, would you come hang out for a little?"

Oliver's eyes widened at the unexpected request. "Sure … yeah," he said, "I can do that."

This wasn't the first time he stepped foot into her apartment, he had been there once before while picking her up to go on one of their summertime adventures, but this was the first time that she had left him in the living room by himself when she went to change out of her Halloween costume and wipe the smudged face paint from her nose. Oliver took a walk around the apartment. He stopped at the fridge where he admired the collection of pictures. Many of them were of Stella, Julie, and the kids. Some pictures looked like they were taken in a photo booth at a work party, and there were also magnets that read words of inspiration like, *"Believe," "Love,"* and, *"Change, it's part of our journey."* His eyes glanced over at her meditation corner, her safe space as she called it. He couldn't explain why or how, but the vibrations of that corner were so vibrant and contagious they instantly calmed his body.

He was pleasantly lost in her world until he felt a nudge at the edge of his pant leg. He looked down to see Simon walking back and forth between his legs, rubbing his back against Oliver's pant leg. "Hey, buddy," Oliver said as he bent down and pet him from head to tail.

Simon returned the gesture with a purr and a lick to his hand.

Oliver walked over to the couch and took his tuxedo jacket off. He sat down and unbuttoned the cuffs of his dress shirt and a few off the top of his collar, making him more comfortable.

Stella reentered the living room in a matching set of lavender-colored pajamas, which he thought fit her personality perfectly. They spent the whole night watching reruns of cheesy sitcoms. One after the other, after the other. Laughter truly was the cure for a broken heart. As time slipped away from them, they both drifted off to sleep on the couch. Oliver woke up a couple hours later to see Stella's head lying peacefully between his chest and shoulder. He knew that there would be no way to move his body without waking her up. Even though he felt his arm tingle, he didn't want to move; instead, he closed his eyes and attempted to fall asleep.

Moments later, Stella awoke. She gently lifted her head and noticed Oliver sitting in what looked like a very uncomfortable position on her couch. She smiled as she studied his face. She liked what she saw. For some reason he appeared to look happier in his sleep, and she also couldn't help but notice that he looked very handsome in a tux. She saw a black tail move from the other side of his arm. She reached her neck over to see Simon curled up against his free arm.

In that moment she caught a wave of clarity. In that moment she saw Oliver, Oliver Roads, and it felt … right. She thought about what it would feel like to kiss him. She then debated whether it was a smart move to make or not, but Stella wasn't shy and the feeling was tempting, so she acted in the moment like she usually did. Life was more fun that way. She carefully brought her face close to his, leaned over and planted a kiss on his cheek. She then whispered to herself, "Maybe it's you." There was a moment of reflection before she softly placed her head back down on his chest, closed her eyes and drifted peacefully back to sleep.

Oliver's eyes shot wide open. *Did that just happen?* he thought. *Holy shit, she just gave me a green light.*

The next morning was a blur. Oliver tried to speak but a whole lot of gibberish came out. Finally, he mustered up the courage to say, "Will you be my girlfriend? I mean go out with me? I mean, yes, yes, will you go out with me ... and be my girlfriend?"

Stella paused for a second, which felt like hours to Oliver. When he didn't think his face could get any redder, she jumped into his arms, gave him a giant hug and a kiss on the lips, which was a bit green on his end, but they would work on that. "Yes!" she exclaimed. "Let's try this!"

Oliver nodded. He then simply turned around and power walked straight to his car. "I'll text you later," he managed to shout back to her.

They had been going strong ever since. They both had something the other longed for; Stella had her heart open to love and the optimism to trust in whatever life had to offer; Oliver had his kind heart and ability to cherish the beauty of an individual. They were perfect together.

~   ~   ~

Hannah ran through the sliding doors of the department store. "Come on, you guys! Walk faster!"

The three of them walked up to a Christmas tree perfectly displayed at the front of the store's entrance. The tree was decorated in a simple row of twinkling white lights. There was bright green and red tinsel wrapped around the evergreen from the trunk to the tip and every branch had a tiny piece of folded card stock tied to it with a white ribbon. Hannah looked at Oliver. "Go on," he said. "Pick one." Hannah reached her arm out and slid a card off of a branch. She opened the card and began to read the print: "My name is Nina, thank you for making this Christmas one to remember. On my wish list this year is a Kimberly Play Doll. Thank you again for making this Christmas special!"

Hannah looked up at Oliver and Stella. "Aren't you going to pick one too?" she asked.

Oliver and Stella each took a card from the tree. They read theirs and then the three of them giddily walked into the store on a mission to buy a present that would make it a wonderful Christmas for a special soul.

The shopping mall was packed with patrons. Christmas was only a few days away and the entire town seemed to be doing some last-minute shopping. Hannah and Stella skipped down the toy doll aisle as they searched for the requested gift.

Oliver went straight to the aisle of board games. He was looking for a game of Memory. He found it too, the last one in the store. As he grabbed the game off of the shelf and began to walk away, he stopped abruptly, concerned by the disheveled shelves. He took a moment to pull merchandise that had been lost in the back of the shelf to the front and then continued to match up the corners and straighten the line of games. He couldn't help it. Stella watched from afar. When she saw what he was doing, she snuck up behind him lovingly and jokingly admired his work. When he had finished, he took a step back and admired it himself. Then a kid came rushing up to the shelf, took one of the board games, observed the box, and then threw it back onto the shelf with not a care in the world. Oliver's eyes grew wide as he reached for the game, but Stella grabbed his hand and led him down another aisle.

The three of them purchased their gifts and headed to a wrapping station where volunteers would help them wrap the toys in colorful Christmas-themed paper and engulf them in festive ribbons and bows. They attached a heartfelt homemade card, double-checking that they wrote the right name down, and placed the gifts in a bin that was labeled, "Santa's Sleigh."

"Nice work!" Stella said as she gave Hannah and Oliver a high five.

"That was so much fun!" Hannah exclaimed. She meant it too.

Stella beamed, this was something she had done every year since she turned sixteen, but this year felt different. It was nice to share an experience like this with Oliver. She had invited people to participate in years past, but no one ever committed. Julie did once but then life got busy with the twins. She knew that Oliver understood how important this event was to her and she loved that when she invited him, he didn't have to think twice. He simply said, "I wouldn't miss it." And Hannah, she was the sweetest. Stella was so happy she got to meet her. Her innocence was pure. Stella saw a piece of herself in Hannah's innocence, for she had been told by many that her essence resembled a child's. But what Stella really enjoyed that evening was seeing how Oliver watched over her. Every time Hannah would run off his eyes would follow her, not to be overbearing but just to be sure he knew she was safe and accounted for. It was subtle and sweet.

Hannah fell in love with Stella, she had never hung out with a girl older than she and it almost felt as though she had a big sister. Every little girl wanted a big sister. Hannah tapped Stella on the arm and asked, "What are you doing tomorrow? Want to come hang out with us?"

"Awe, I would love to," she said, flattered, and she meant it, "but I have a church concert tomorrow."

"A church concert?" Oliver asked, confused.

"Yeah, for the holiday!"

This was the first time that Oliver had heard about this concert, plus he was a bit taken aback that she went to church. He could have just said that, but instead the words, "I didn't think you believed in God," flew out.

"What made you think that?" she asked.

"'Cause you're so—" he searched for the right word "—spiritual. Don't they kind of contradict each other?"

"I believe in God, the universe, angels, everything. I've felt them all my life!" Her face lit up every time she spoke of the energy of the universe or anything similar. It was almost impossible for it not to.

Hannah said, "My brother doesn't believe in God. He's an atheist."

Oliver stood there blushing again. This was the second blunt comment that had so easily floated out of Hannah's six-year-old mouth that night and he hoped there wouldn't be anymore. He was baffled that she even knew the word atheist. "Not totally," he defended; then he caved. "Okay, maybe I'm a little bit of an atheist." Then he began to ramble and was unable to stop. "It's just hard to believe that, with such a powerful God, there is so much hurt and broken people in this world. You know?"

Stella placed her hand on his shoulder. "It's okay that you don't believe, Oliver," she said.

"Really?" he questioned.

"Yes," she said, and he could feel that she meant it. "Beliefs are based off of what we experience, and everybody has their own experiences. See we are constantly living new adventures that change our perspective; that is one of the reasons why beliefs are always changing. On a side note…"

Oliver let out a small chuckle. She did this "side note" thing a lot recently, a habit he didn't think she was aware of. It happened mid-conversation; he became accustomed to it and found it rather adorable.

She continued, "I hope this never happens to you, but one day, if your world shatters and you have no one to turn to, you may find…" She paused; her ears pricked up as though she was listening for the right word to be whispered into her ear. "Comfort," she continued, "comfort in knowing that whoever's in charge up there or energetically in this world or wherever will listen to what you have to say and may just give you exactly what you need."

Oliver stared into Stella's eyes, which were glowing with passion. He was once again mesmerized by her spirit, her light, which flowed through her being. "You were right," is all he could say.

"Huh? I don't get it."

"When I first met you. You said, 'What's not to like?'"

Stella smiled. "I did?"

"Yep. And you were right. There is nothing not to like. You are perfect."

Stella was quite aware that she was far from perfect, but she could tell that Oliver spoke his truth and those words made her heart melt over and over again. The way he looked at her, like she was an angel placed on this earth, like a song worth singing, like a reason to be living, it felt right. All of it. They shared a kiss. This time Hannah didn't say, "Eww," she simply smiled in admiration and said, "So this concert tomorrow, are we going?"

# Silent Night

It was Christmas Eve and the white stone church on the edge of town was filled with families, all of them dressed to the nines in their holiday attire. Kyle and the twins sat in the pews with the rest of the congregation enjoying the songs sung by the choir and, much to Julie's and Kyle's relief, the twins seemed to be very well behaved that evening. It may have been a gift in the spirit of Christmas, or perhaps it was the cookies Kyle snuck into his pocket to bribe them with. Either way, well behaved, pleasant twins were music to their ears.

The church choir stood next to a beautifully decorated tree, which twinkled; next to them stood a nicely lit display of the nativity scene. Stella and Julie stood in the alto section of the choir. The baritones stood behind them and the sopranos placed themselves adjacent. Julie looked out into the pews. She smiled at Kyle and the twins and then blew them a kiss.

The choir sang classical and elegant songs of Christmas. They sang "Drummer Boy," "Away in a Manger", and Stella's favorite, "Mary, Did You know".

Stella couldn't help but smile when she saw Oliver and Hannah enter the church doors mid-concert. They found a nice spot in the second to last pew and managed to do so without being disruptive. The fact that they showed up meant everything to her.

The house lights of the church gently disappeared as the ushers made their way down the pews handing out a tiny candle to each member of the congregation. The entire congregation then stood in their pew, candles lit, and sang in unison the elegant words of "Silent Night". Oliver stopped singing and looked out into the still and peaceful sight of the congregation. He closed his eyes and couldn't help but feel the powerful rush of such an elegant song, and when he opened his eyes again, he admired the dance of each glistening flame. Words couldn't describe exactly what happened in that moment, but the experience of it all sent a warm tickle up his spine. And then Stella broke away from the choir and sang a solo he'd never forget.

~   ~   ~

When the service was over, Stella and the rest of the choir stood outside of the church and greeted the congregation. Stella gave Julie an enormous hug.

"We have to run," Julie said. "Looks like these kids are ready to go to bed."

Stella looked over to see Kyle holding a sleeping Geri in his arms and Ryan, thumb in mouth, holding on to his dad's pant leg.

"Okay, bye, bye, see you later." Stella waved.

Still gripping his father's pant leg, Ryan managed to remove his thumb from his mouth for a split second in order to wave goodbye back to her.

As Julie and her family walked toward the car, she spotted Oliver. "Hey Oliver, thank you for coming."

"Of course. You did great."

"You flatter me," she joked as she continued to walk. "Merry Christmas!"

"Merry Christmas," he replied as he approached Stella, Hannah following close to his side. "You did great too," he said as he presented Stella with a bouquet of red roses.

"Thank you for coming and thank you for these." She held them up to her nose and inhaled, enjoying the aroma. "They're beautiful."

"You're welcome. What are your plans for the rest of the night?" he asked.

"Um, nothing really. Thought I'd go home … see what's open, maybe grab some food on the way."

"Why don't you come over for dinner?" Hannah chimed in.

Stella looked up at Oliver, awaiting his reaction.

"Yes, come. Please. My family would be really happy to officially meet you."

"Meet your parents?" She proceeded with caution. "Are you sure about that?"

"Yes," he said confidently, "My mom will be super nice and normal and my dad, well, he will be pleased to know I'm not making you up," he joked. "Please come."

Stella laughed too. "Dinner sounds great."

And then she hopped into her car and followed Oliver and Hannah to the Roads house for a Christmas Eve feast.

# Family and a Feast

Hannah charged into the kitchen of the Roads house. She shouted with excitement, "Mom, Dad, Stella's here!"

"What?" Grace said as she pulled a roast out of the oven careful not to burn herself.

Jack's ears pricked up at the sound of Hannah's news. He turned his head towards the hallway, but before he could say anything Oliver appeared at the door with Stella at his side.

"Hi," Grace managed to say as she tried her best to pretend that she wasn't still processing this wonderful yet unprecedented moment.

Stella smiled. She appeared very calm on the outside, though inside her heart was racing. "It's nice to meet you. You have a lovely home," she said and boy did she mean it. The Roads house was exactly the kind of home she always dreamed of living in. From the outside it looked warm, inviting and perfect, like it came straight off a holiday postcard. The inside was a perfect match. Stella noticed that a tremendous amount of thought had been placed into the design of each room. Each room elegantly put together and frosted with family photos that hung on the wall, which were a beautiful reminder of the occupants within. Every element was placed with attention. It was clear to Stella that Mrs. Roads had made this house a home.

"Thank you," Grace said.

After an awkward silence, Oliver chimed in, "We invited Stella to dinner. Is that okay?"

"Of course it is! Yes, please, make yourself at home."

Still stunned, Jack managed to hop off of the couch. "I'll set another plate," he volunteered. That was Stella, he remembered her from the swim meet, cheering in the bleachers. He had a hunch at the time but promised Grace that he wouldn't press the issue so part of him still thought she was made up until this moment. Boy was he wrong and happy to be. His son may have gotten the prettiest girl in town. Jack couldn't help but think that maybe Oliver did have a little bit of his old man in him. He beamed with pride all through dinner, barely blinking. He wanted to remember everything about that night.

It was a good thing that Grace was there. She had an entire repertoire of entertainer's manners. She could keep a conversation going with anyone in any kind of circumstance. She asked Stella all about her upbringing; though it was heavy Stella shared with an open heart and somehow managed to make it seem happier than it must have been. Grace asked her about school, her hopes and dreams, and they even talked about her cat, which made Hannah happy because she desperately wanted a pet, but

Mrs. Roads had continued to put her foot down on that one.

Mrs. Roads made Stella feel like she was a part of the family like a daughter. She asked all the kinds of questions that parents asked their kids in movies. She seemed genuinely interested in her life and Stella was a magnificent reader of energy. She could tell Mrs. Roads was just as warm at her core as the home she led. The food was fantastic; the company was captivating. And Stella was completely filled full with happiness.

"Would you like some more potatoes?" Grace asked as she began to clear the serving dishes from the center of the table.

"Oh, no thank you," Stella replied as she placed her hands on her full tummy. "This food is delicious, but I'm beyond full."

"Well, I hope you saved room for dessert," Jack said, which was the first full sentence he'd said throughout the entire meal; it seemed that the shock was finally wearing off.

"Mom makes the best apple pie," Hannah gushed.

"I do," Grace admitted as she reentered the dining room with a warm apple pie in her hands.

Oliver turned towards Stella, he leaned in. "She really does," he confirmed. The two shared a smile as the luscious scent of melted cinnamon sugar and crisp fresh apples amongst a warm buttered dough filled the air.

Stella turned to Grace. "There is always room for dessert," she said, beaming.

Grace placed a slice of pie on every plate. She added a scoop of vanilla ice cream to everyone's pie except Oliver's and Jack's; for some reason, one that the girls would never be able to understand, they preferred their pie without ice cream. Grace handed a plate to Hannah. "Sweetie, pass this down, please."

One bite of the pie and Stella's taste buds melted. It was fantastic. "That was delicious, Mrs. Roads. The best I've ever tasted, no question."

"I'm glad you enjoyed it," Grace said as she reached her hand out and placed it lovingly on Stella's forearm. "I can give you the recipe if you'd like."

Stella had only been there a couple of hours, but she felt like she belonged. If there was such a thing as a perfect night, this would be it.

Jack looked over at Oliver with pride. He chimed into the conversation once more. "Will you be staying for games?"

"Games?" she asked.

"Tonight is game night," Oliver said.

"It's a Christmas Eve tradition!" Hannah cheered, unable to contain her excitement.

"Oh, I don't know," Stella said. "I have to work early in the morning, the life of a retail employee."   Even though it was a holiday she didn't mind working; in fact, she volunteered to work every holiday that the store remained open. She adored her co-workers and spending time with them actually made the holiday more fun. It was better than sitting inside by herself or going to Julie's; she was, of course, always welcome but sometimes she felt too much like a guest. Tonight, her heart wanted to stay longer at the Roads house. They had been so welcoming to her she didn't want to offend, nor did she want to overstay her welcome. Oliver sensed her hesitation. He leaned over to her and whispered, "You should stay. It will be fun."

If Oliver wanted her to stay, then why wouldn't she? "Alright, maybe just one game," she said.

A game night with the Roads family was unlike anything Stella had witnessed before and nothing like she had imagined it to be. They preferred mind games over cards and the competition was very much alive. The whole family sat around the living room, they played taboo, catch phrase, and charades. Jack, Grace, and Hannah roared with laughter and cheer. They became playfully aggressive, they called each other out when one may have accidently slipped up on a rule and used a "rhymed with". Oliver, though quiet compared to his family, managed to join in on the laughter and passionate pleas. Stella adored seeing him break out of his shell a bit. Even if it was only a little, it was another side of him and that was wonderful.

When the girls won the final round of charades, Hannah leapt from her seat. "We won! We won!" she screamed as she ran around the room.

"You must have cheated!" Jack declared as he joined in on the fun.

"Did not!" Hannah yelled back as she jumped into his arms. Jack tickled her until she broke away with laughter.

Stella glanced over at Oliver who wore a smile on his face the entire time. He sensed her stare and when he turned towards her she whispered, "It's past my bedtime. I should be headed home."

Oliver stood up. "I'll walk you out."

Jack stood too. He held his hand out towards Stella. "Stella," he said, "it was great meeting you." He had a firm and sincere hand shake, just as she'd expected.

Grace gave her a giant hug, which was warm and safe, just as she'd expected it to be. It lasted longer than Stella anticipated, which caught her slightly off guard, and for a brief moment the vanilla fragrance Grace wore sent her on a journey. Stella felt her arms hug Grace back, squeezing tightly. Stella closed her eyes, lost in the moment. Her emotions began to build, her nose began to sniffle, but Grace didn't let go. She held her tighter and gave her a motherly rub up and down the curve of her back. "Honey, you are welcome here any time."

Oliver basked in this moment; the night couldn't have gone any better. "Okay Mom," he said.

Grace released Stella from the embrace. She too wiped tears from her eyes, for the embrace had been more healing and powerful than she had expected. "Sorry." She blushed. "Any time. I mean it."

Oliver intertwined his hands with Stella's and walked her to the door. They grabbed their jackets from the coat rack and exited the Roads house. Jack placed his arm around Grace. "I like her," she said.

"Me too," Jack agreed.

Hannah's rush of energy had run out as she now napped pleasantly on the couch.

~ ~ ~

Oliver and Stella walked down the circular driveway of the Roads house. The snow had stopped falling for the night though it covered the grass in a dream-like blanket of white. The Christmas lights twinkled behind them as the fresh air stood still. Oliver placed both of his arms around her. The bridge of their noses rested upon one another's. "This night was perfect," he said.

She smiled. "Your family is great. I love them," she said.

Oliver couldn't help but smile, which was almost always followed with a blush. He preferred to blame his rouge cheeks on the cold instead of actually admitting how happy he felt when he heard the words 'I love them' fall from her lips. "Well, they love you too," he said. "Believe me; I've never seen my dad be that nice to anyone before."

Stella laughed. "Ah, my cheeks hurt. I can't stop smiling."

"I love it when you smile."

She slowly opened her eyes to meet his. "Corny," she said in complete amusement.

Oliver leaned in for a kiss. Their lips touched, sending a shiver down her spine. Their kiss gradually became more passionate.

Oliver held her close. Once again, their eyes closed as they enjoyed the comforting heat of the moment, neither one wanting this moment to end. "I have to go," she said reluctantly. "Okay," he finally caved.

He released her from his embrace. Stella began to walk to her car, which was parked on the side of the road. "Hey!" Oliver shouted.

Stella turned to look at him.

"Text me when you're home."

Stella smiled as her eyes exuded a new level of pure joy. And with her clever wit and charm she said, "I love you too."

Like a scene from the movies the snow began to fall once again. Stella hopped into her car and drove off down the road. Oliver stood in the driveway, unable to move, his heart in pure bliss. There is a sensation that some people speak about.

It's a feeling so wonderful, so sensational, so magnificent, and that feeling is knowing that the person you fell in love with also loves you back.

# SPRING

# A Love We Deserve

Springtime in Oklahoma was filled with gloom, overcast skies and rain, lots of it. Oliver loved the rain, Stella did too. She always said that the droplets of water brought change and cleansing to the world; a fresh start. Proof once again of her positive outlook on life, which may have started to rub off on Oliver, if only a little.

The sky was dark gray, and the rain poured from the clouds striking the side of the garage where Oliver stood speechless. "So, what do you think?" Jack asked as he unveiled the newly remodeled garage, which was now completely transformed into a fully functional gym. "We've got weight machines there. Bands, ropes, a tire! Cardio over there in the corner. Our own home gym! What do you think?"

*I think you lost your mind*, Oliver thought, though he obviously didn't say that. He knew what his dad was doing. He was trying to create something they could bond over; unfortunately this was very one-sided, but Oliver didn't want to rain on his father's excitement, so he forced a smile and nodded in approval.

Jack knew this wasn't Oliver's idea of a good time, but he thought it might be useful because he wasn't confident in that area. Perhaps now that his son's confidence seemed to grow with Stella, maybe, just maybe he would be open to expanding that confidence in other areas like the gym. Jack was fully prepared to take this opportunity to try once again to create a bond with his son. He knew personally the benefit of lifting weights not only for the physical build but also for the internal strength it seemed to build simultaneously. Showing Oliver the gym could have gone many different ways, and even though he wasn't oblivious to Oliver's internal reaction he still thought this reveal seemed to be going better than he planned. Jack patted Oliver on the back. "This will be good for us. You and me, bonding. A father-son workout. I'm excited!" he said.

~ ~ ~

Stella stood behind the counter of a boutique flower shop called L'amour de la fleur. Since her school schedule became more intense in the last semester, she was forced to move on from the department store and landed a job at the local flower shop. She still kept in contact with her old co-workers but had to admit that working at the flower shop was a better fit. This job gave her a sense of joy and fulfillment. The flowers were beautiful, and even though she spent the days between four walls, the aroma was enough to transport her mind onto more wondrous adventure, plus she really enjoyed the creativity that came with creating the floral arrangements. She found happiness arose within her every time a patron came in to pick up their bouquet.

She stood at the counter arranging blue tulips with white roses and a green garnish into a beautiful bouquet destined for a baby shower as Geri and Ryan played hide and seek while Julie attempted small talk with Stella. "How do you like it here?" she asked.

"I love it! The hours work better around my school schedule and, besides, who doesn't want to be around flowers all day? They are a constant reminder of how beautiful life can be."

"That's sweet," Julie said sarcastically. Her voice dropped into a serious tone. "Hey, can I ask you something?"

"Of course. What's up?"

Julie looked back and forth to make sure the kids weren't lingering in the corner. She whispered to Stella, "Do you think Kyle would leave me?"

"What?" Stella asked, confused by this question which to her seemed to come out of left field. "Did something happen?"

"No, no, nothing happened. The thought has just crossed my mind recently." And then Julie began to pour her heart out. "You know I'm a bit bossy and controlling and that's who I've always been. I just don't want it to become too much for him."

Julie looked at Stella and for the first time in their entire relationship Stella saw doubt, fear, and a pinch of guilt and uncertainty occupy her friend's eyes.

"Julie," she said with compassion, "I don't think you have anything to worry about. Kyle loves you."

"Yes," she said, unconvinced.

"He does!"

"I guess you're right." She began to cave.

"I am right," Stella assured her, "so much that he wants another baby with you."

"Which I keep vetoing," she pointed out.

The two stood in silence. Then finally Stella spoke. "If you're feeling a little … bad about the way you treat him, maybe plan a night. Just the two of you. Oh, bring him flowers!" she said as she passionately held up the perfectly arranged bouquet.

Julie laughed a genuine laugh for the first time in this entire conversation.

"I'm serious," Stella continued, "show him how much he means to you. The spark is still there. I promise you that."

Julie looked over towards Stella, she smiled with pride. "When did you get so wise?"

Stella shrugged. Julie sniffled up some of her emotion. "How are you and Oliver?" she asked. "Still going strong?"

Stella's face lit up at the thought of Oliver. "Yep, I love him."

Julie's eyes beamed with excitement. Stella had used that word before but not like this. Julie could tell this relationship was different than her previous ones. There wasn't another Oliver and there wasn't another Stella.

"But these past few months, I almost feel…" Stella's face dropped slightly with concern as she searched for the words. "I don't know. I feel like something is coming."

"Good things?" Julie asked.

Stella shook her head no. "I don't know," she continued. "Maybe it's just my own fear. I don't want to lose him. I never would have pictured us together, but we balance each other out. Sometimes it just seems too good, you know?"

"Aw honey," Julie said as she placed her hand on Stella's, "your heart has been through enough pain. You deserve a love like Oliver's. That man is not going anywhere; he's never going to break your heart. I'm sure of that. He adores you."

Stella smiled. The words Julie spoke mirrored her truth. Stella didn't see him going anywhere, but still there was this feeling of uncertainty that she couldn't seem to shake.

# Groovy Kind of Love

Rain once again poured from the sky. The heavy drops smashed against the tall windows of the library. It was late in the evening and Stella had visited the library after class in order to get some studying done. Her books were sprawled across the desk. She studied intensely the cognitive path of addiction. Her eyes fell tired of looking at the small print and her brain barely recognized the concepts anymore. Each sentence quickly became just letters on the page that made their way in and out of her brain without leaving a trace. Then her phone dinged with a text from Oliver that read, I'm here.

Stella gathered up her books and rushed down the stairs of the library. When she exited the double doors, she saw Oliver looking handsome as ever in jeans and a dark green T-shirt with a casual, yet sophisticated, well-fit, gray zipper jacket. He leaned against the side of the car holding a black umbrella in one hand to shield him from the rain and a cardboard drink tray in the other, which held two coffees, one for Stella and one for Oliver.

He smiled at the sight of her. Umbrella in hand he began to take a step towards her so she wouldn't have to get soaked by the rain, but before he became close, Stella had already stepped out into the rain and ran straight towards him. She placed her hands on his chest and gave him a kiss. "What was that for?" he asked, not complaining but curious. Her spontaneity was something he learned to enjoy. Something he was not.

"No reason. Just wanted to kiss you."

He couldn't help but blush once again. He loved everything about her. He loved how her pupils grew big every time she looked at him, how her face lit up every time a corny, cute, adorable phrase floated from her mouth. She knew how clever she was, it was one of her many superpowers. Stella was unlike any girl he had ever met before. Not only was she completely confident in who she was and in every move that she made, she also seemed to love him. Flaws and all. And to be accepted as we are … is there a greater display of love?

For some reason all his quirks that made him weird, an outcast, undesirable in the eyes of some, she seemed to cherish. She was a special soul; he was mesmerized. Every time he saw her his heart seemed to flutter. He didn't understand exactly how this all came to be his reality or what she saw in him, but it didn't matter. They were in love and it worked.

"I got you a coffee," he said as they kissed again under his umbrella. He opened her car door. "Hop on in." She took a seat as he gently shut the door and ran to the driver's side. He sat down and brushed the droplets of rain off of his shoulder. Together they drove off down the road.

~ ~ ~

That night, Stella and Oliver lay cuddled up on the couch. The rain hit the windows for hours creating a calming melody, perfect weather for a movie. They alternated movies all through the night and found themselves gently closing their eyes and drifting off to sleep.

A couple hours later, Stella awoke to a roll of thunder followed by a flash of lightning. She was reminded briefly of a story one of her foster parents told her years ago when she was small and the thunder made her cry. The nice woman said, "No need to be scared. Thunder is just God bowling." As silly as it was, she had very sweet dreams that night. She dreamt of a figure without a face, just an illumination of white. They were standing side by side, bowling.

Stella glanced over at Oliver whose eyes gently began to open. He let out a yawn as he stretched his arms above him.

"What time is it?" she asked.

Oliver looked over at the alarm clock on his table. "Almost midnight."

"I have to go home," she said and yawned.

He leaned his head closer to hers. "No, stay here," he begged.

Though she wanted to stay she had to resist. "I can't," she said, "I have a test tomorrow."

"I can drive you to school in the morning. It's no trouble."

She knew he meant it when he told her that it was no trouble, but her class was early and she didn't want to wake him. "My house is closer to school," she reasoned, "and I could use the extra time in the morning to study. Besides, I sleep better at my place."

Oliver knew that nothing would convince her to stay. She made valid points, but he also knew that there was one she wasn't going to elaborate on. Every night since she adopted him Simon had slept with her and that night would be no different. Even when Oliver stayed the night at her place, Simon would gently make his way over their bodies, settle in between the two of them, and purr loudly in endless comfort. "Okay," Oliver said. He opened his eyes. "Give me a sec. I'll drive you."

"No," she said, "you're sleepy. I'll drive myself."

He wished he would have been the one to insist again; however, he was exhausted. "You sure?"

"Yes."

"The keys are on the table," he said.

Stella gave him a kiss on the cheek. "Goodnight," she whispered. Then she walked to the table across the room.

"Stella?" he said.

She turned. "Yeah?"

"Make sure you text me when you're home."

Each time he said that she couldn't help but feel a sense of comfort. Those words from his lips were a constant reminder of their conversation that day in the diner; a constant reminder that she was loved. "I will," she said.

"Drive safe," he said under his breath as he drifted back to sleep.

"I will," she whispered before exiting the house.

~ ~ ~

The rain had slowed to a slight drizzle. Stella drove Oliver's car through the quiet abandoned streets. "A Groovy Kind of Love" came on the radio. She loved Phil Collins, who doesn't? Every song was catchy and magical. He had a way with words. She couldn't help but sway back and forth in her seat as she sang along.

The streetlight turned to red and she slowed the car to a stop. She turned up the volume slightly and continued to get lost in the feelings of the tune.

When the street light turned green, her foot pressed down on the accelerator. As she pulled forward into the intersection a car came out of nowhere. It sped down the wet road, ran the red light, and crashed directly into the driver's side of Stella's car.

Sirens rushed down the road and the streets filled with first responders flashing their blue and red lights. Both drivers remained unconscious.

~~~

It was a night like no other, Julie and Kyle hadn't been intimate in quite some time. When one would be in the mood the other would fall asleep from pure exhaustion due to a day of activities. Something had been missing in their marriage for a while. They were always preoccupied, always on the go and therefore with the chaos of life it was easy to go unnoticed. But when the night fell, and they had to sit in minutes of silence it was painfully obvious that they weren't the young lovers they once were.

This night was different. After her talk with Stella, Julie was determined to reignite the spark between her and Kyle. That evening, she surprised him with a date night without the twins. Her mother had agreed to watch the kids overnight so Julie and Kyle could not only have a wonderful, romantic and much needed evening out on the town, but they also wouldn't have to end it early once they arrived back home. This was a night that was long overdue.

A bouquet of red roses rested in the vase on the night stand as Kyle and Julie fell back into bed. They panted in elation. "I can't believe we just did that!" Kyle exclaimed as he lifted his arm for Julie to come close. The two snuggled underneath the covers.

Julie laughed. "It's been a while." It had been a long time since she had felt her husband inside her and she had to admit she'd missed him. This night was an important step in bringing them back together.

"And then you bought me flowers, took me to dinner," he raved. "Not that I don't love this but … where is this coming from?"

Julie twiddled her fingers across his chest. "I just wanted to do something special for you."

Kyle looked into her eyes, he felt her tremble. "Julie, what's going on?" he asked. "I'm not buying it."

"Okay," she said as she took a deep breath in and out to calm her nerves. This wasn't the conversation she wanted to have, especially after such a magical night. But maybe the universe knew better and was creating a much-needed conversation. Emotional intimacy was just as important as physical intimacy and they both had been equally absent. She supposed now was as good a time as any to have a discussion about what she'd been feeling. "I've just felt kind of bad about how I treat you." She continued, "I know I'm a little demanding and aggressive"—the words started to pour out of her mouth—"and I realize that sometimes I don't give you the recognition you deserve, I kind of take you for granted and at times I steal your pants from you."

"What?"

"Figuratively speaking."

"Oh."

She continued, "I just want you to know that I love you and I love the life we created together and I'm going to change," she assured him, "I'm going to try to be more considerate."

Julie said her piece and, as unpolished as the delivery was, it felt like a weight had been lifted off of her shoulders. She looked up at Kyle. He stared silently back at her. She became nervous. *What was he going to say? How was he going to react to everything she just said? Would he be angry? Was this the end? Was he just in shock?* Her thoughts gravitated towards negativity incredibly quickly, so much that she wished she could rewind time and take it all back. Then suddenly, much to her surprise, Kyle started to laugh.

"Why? Why are you laughing?" she asked, confused and genuinely concerned.

Kyle used his fingers to gently brush the hair out of her eyes and tucked it behind her ear. He looked her directly in the eye and said, "Julie, I don't want you to change anything about you."

"Really?" she asked in pure disbelief.

"Yes. You are bossy and demanding and will always speak your mind, even if no one asked you."

Julie didn't know where he was going with this. It sounded cruel.

Kyle continued, "But all of those traits are what I love most about you."

Julie's eyes began to fill with tears.

"Maybe we haven't been 'us' for a while, but that's on both of us. You are exactly the woman I fell in love with. The woman I am in love with."

"Really?"

"Yes."

Julie looked into his eyes and could tell that he meant every word.

"Sure, a lot of guys may not be able to handle it, but I kind of like you wearing my pants," he joked.

Julie joined in on the laughter. "God, I love you," she said as she leaned in for another kiss. The passion continued when suddenly her phone started to ring. Julie hopped up.

"You're going to answer it?" Kyle asked, cursing the timing.

"It's one in the morning," she said, "at our age nobody calls people at one in the morning unless it's important."

She answered the call. "Hello. Yes, this is she." Within seconds Julie's face fell pale.

"Julie, what's wrong?" Kyle asked. "Julie?"

Julie stood in pure shock. She could barely mumble the words, "I'll be right there," into the phone.

~  ~  ~

Julie rushed to the hospital. Time seemed to slow and became a blur. A nurse took her down a never-ending hallway. She finally stopped in front of a room where through a door frame her eyes could see Stella, bloody, unconscious, and hooked up to machines. The doctors worked diligently for hours. Her knees fell weak and she collapsed in the hallway of the hospital.

# Eight Days

Eight 'X's marked the passing of eight days. Stella lay in the hospital; though her body seemed to be healing her essence was lost in a coma.

The night of the accident was a blur to Oliver. The police ran the registration of the car and instantly came knocking on the door of the Roads house.

Grace's heart sank when she answered the door and saw two police officers with sorrow in their eyes. A mix of emotions ran through her head that night, all negative except for one, a brief wave of relief that her son wasn't also in the car. She figured every mother would have that thought if, God forbid, they ever found themselves in such a situation, but she couldn't help but feel guilty too. She hated that a thought like that even crossed her mind to begin with, but it did.

Grace was the one who woke Oliver and told him the news. She would never forget his face of shock, disbelief, and helplessness. It was now permanently engraved in her memory. He was in too much shock to drive, and she didn't want him to be alone, so she took him to the hospital that night. Jack tried to insist that he went along too, but Grace instructed him to stay at home with Hannah. She was still sound asleep in her room. It just wasn't the time to tell her. This all happened so suddenly; they needed more time to process it. They needed more information. It was better that she slept.

Oliver stayed at the hospital day and night for eight days straight. Julie entered Stella's room to see him sitting next to Stella, who still lay in a coma. "Still here," she stated the obvious.

Oliver barely looked up. "Where else would I be?"

Julie pulled up a chair and took a seat across from him.

"Do you think she's going to wake up?" Oliver asked.

"It's been eight days in a coma. The doctors don't seem that optimistic."

Oliver asked again, this time with a forceful tone and direct eye contact that caught Julie off guard. "Yeah, but do **you** think she's going to wake up?"

She thought for a moment as she chose her words carefully. "I pray every day," she said. "Even if she does wake up, at this point, they say her chances of making a moderate recovery are less than ten percent." Julie glanced towards Stella as she dropped her head and sighed. "I don't know what's worse, passing before one's time or living life part vegetable."

Oliver squeezed his eyes tight, he attempted to drown out his thoughts but it was impossible. "I should have driven her that night," he confessed, "then none of this would have happened." As much as he tried to hold in his tears they began to fall from his eyes and stream like a river down his cheek.

"Don't say that," Julie said sternly.

"It's true."

"You don't know that. Had you been in the car you might be lying right next to her."

"I wish I was!" he shouted.

Oliver's words released from his mouth and hit Julie hard. She loved Stella too; she knew how hard he was hurting, how much pain he must be in, but running the train of regret is an impossible gain, especially the ones we don't have to claim. "Go home, Oliver," she said gently. "Get some rest."

"I'm going to stay the night," he insisted.

"You've stayed enough nights. Take this one off. I'll be here."

That night Oliver went home. Though he didn't want to leave he knew it would be good for him. He felt peace of mind knowing that Julie would be by her side. The important thing was that Stella would have someone there in case she woke up.

~ ~ ~

He had to admit the hot water from the shower was refreshing. The water streamed down his body, washing away the soot of this reality. When he stepped out and dried himself off, he felt better. It almost felt like all this was a horrible nightmare and that things would be back to normal. But they weren't.

He lay on his bed, his eyes glued to the ceiling. Grace entered the room. "How are you feeling?" she asked.

Without blinking he said, "You really have to ask that?"

Grace walked over to him and took a seat on his bed. The truth was she didn't know how to talk to Oliver about this. She wondered if any mother would. She had actually searched the internet for insight and advice, but in the moment she seemed to forget it all. Every time she spoke with him, she felt as though she was walking on egg shells. Her son was fragile, understandably so. But she tried her best. "I understand this is a difficult situation. If you want to talk, I'm here for you. Okay?"

Oliver remained still and silent. Grace said what she needed to say and that was all she could do. Just let him know she was there whenever he felt the desire to communicate. She stood up and was making her way to the door when suddenly he said, "I'm not ready to give up on her, Mom."

Grace's heart filled with a tiny light. This was the most he had opened up to her since the accident. "Maybe say a little prayer." She suggested.

Oliver scoffed. "To what?" he asked. "To whom?"

Grace raised both of her kids in church, but Oliver never continued once he turned eighteen. Grace was a believer, but she knew that Oliver had never really believed in much.

"To all of them, God, the angels, the universe, the stars. To whoever will listen. To whoever you turn to when your world is breaking and you don't know what else to do."

Grace exited the room and Oliver took a moment to sit with his mother's advice. It sounded familiar. Even he couldn't believe what he did next. He rolled off of the bed, fell to his knees and prayed.

Oliver prayed and prayed and prayed.

~ ~ ~

The next morning, he walked into the hospital. He looked, felt, and smelled better than before. Emotionally he was much more composed than the night before. He held a beautiful bouquet of pink tulips, Stella's favorite flower. As he entered her room, Julie stood up. "Good morning," he said.

"Hi," she said timidly. She pointed to the tulips. "Are those for Stella?"

"Yeah, from her co-workers."

"That's sweet," Julie said. She tried hard to keep from crying. "Hey Oliver, we need to talk."

Oliver read the change in her tone and within a moment of her eyes meeting his, his face lost its light.

Julie sat him down and began to explain what he already knew. She was going to give up on Stella. She explained to him that it wasn't an easy decision; in fact, it was the hardest decision she ever had to make, but at this point it might be what was best for her soul. She wasn't quite ready to do it now. She said she would give it a couple days to really sink in, make sure she was doing the right thing. "Tuesday," she said, like it was any old item on a to-do list.

Oliver heard every word that fell from her lips. He didn't seem to react. He immediately exited the room and walked home in a trance. He would continue to walk around like a zombie for the days that led up to her demise. He was very much on autopilot, which was kind of how he lived his life before Stella anyway. In a weird way, it was comfortable because it was familiar.

~    ~    ~

That night, the Roads family sat around the table attempting to enjoy their dinner. Oliver sat in silence and barely touched his food. He lasted about fifteen minutes before picking up his plate and walking it into the kitchen. He made his way up the stairs and back to self-isolation.

The next thing the Roads family heard was that horrible sound of the vacuum. "I'm worried about him," Grace said.

Jack was too.

# Power of Prayer

D ays went by. Oliver didn't know what to do so, therefore, by habit his life fell back into his comfortable routine. He vacuumed the rug, dusted his frames, and attempted to draw, though once again inspiration seemed hard to find. He spent more time staring at a blank piece of paper than he ever had before. Eventually he would get frustrated, crumple the paper and toss it into the trash.

He cussed at God, or whoever was listening. He cussed a lot as he paced back and forth in his room and flipped him off in anger. When the rush of anger was released, the tears of regret would rush in and calmness would fall across his body as he surrendered. He dropped to his knees and began to pray. He didn't know why he did it. It just felt right. This pattern went on for hours.

The next day, as he vacuumed, he accidently pulled a little too hard on the cord causing the plug to pull out of the socket. He walked over to the socket and as he aggressively pushed it back in, his phone rang. It was Julie. He answered the call and in that moment all the life and joy rushed back into his world!

~ ~ ~

The nurse brought Oliver to the room where Stella sat up awake. She was tired but alert. He watched her in awe from the window. There she was. *Perhaps there is power in prayer,* he thought.

Another nurse walked out of the room. "She's a bit slow at the moment, but the fact that she's awake and in recovery is a miracle in itself."

Oliver shared a smile with the nurse. "Does she remember the accident?" he asked.

"No, nothing leading up to it either. But she knows her friend, so this is a good sign. You can go in and see her now." The nurse walked away down the hallway.

"Thank you."

Julie sat in a chair next to Stella's bed. Kyle stood behind her. Kyle had been a rock for Julie throughout this entire situation. As horrible as this incident was it had brought them closer to one another—a reminder of what was truly important.

Oliver glanced in the room and saw Stella smile. She seemed to be in high spirits, lighting up the room once again.

Julie leaned in towards Stella. "Now that the coast is clear … look who I snuck in!" She leaned down and pulled out Simon from her oversized tote bag.

Simon meowed at the sight of Stella. Her jaw dropped in surprise and joy. Cats have an excellent ability to read energy; therefore Simon could sense that she wasn't one hundred percent well. He crawled up to her side, careful not to cause her body any more pain. He cuddled up to her and gently rested his head on her chest as he licked her hand.

"Julie?" Kyle said, stunned.

"What?" she said innocently.

Kyle didn't continue. Truth be told he was kind of pleased with her audacity.

Oliver entered the room. "Stella!" he said, smiling wide. "I can't believe this! I'm so happy to see you!" He had imagined how this moment would go over and over in his head. He repeated it the entire drive over to the hospital. How great it would feel when they were able to see each other again, how tragedy makes us realize just how much we cherish the ones we love and how their love could grow forward, since time is not promised and therefore always of the essence. But, unfortunately, nothing like this happened. It was clear to Oliver that nothing would play out the way he had imagined. Instead, Stella looked his way with glass eyes. She then looked over to Julie. "Stella, you remember Oliver."

Stella shook her head.

"He's your boyfriend," she said lightly as though her not making the connection was an honest mistake.

Oliver took a step towards her. "Stella, I—" But before he could finish Stella gasped in fear. Oliver stopped in his tracks. Julie and Kyle looked at him too, neither one of them knowing what to do.

Oliver saw Stella, the beautiful, charming, spiritual weirdo he met that past summer. His best friend and the woman he loved. But Stella didn't see him. All she saw was a stranger. He was nothing to her; neither a memory nor a feeling of familiarity. It was as though he never existed. Oliver could not have described how much it pained him in that moment. It was all so unexpected. He saw the frustration and fear in her eyes as she tried to remember any trace of who he was, but she couldn't.

He noticed the tears of defeat that began to weld together in her eyes. He knew he had to leave. He didn't want to cause her any more pain. Honestly, he was just grateful that someone, something, had listened to his prayers, kind of. Stella loved life. She loved to live. And here she was given another chance to do just that. It took everything within him to swallow every word he yearned to say. Instead he said, "I just came here to bring you this." He held up a copy of The Wizard of Oz.

Stella's face glowed once again. "That's my favorite movie!" she exclaimed.

Oliver let out a nervous chuckle. Her excitement, it was the purest thing he'd ever heard, still childlike and innocent. "I know," he said. He tried his best to hold his composure. "I thought you might find it comforting during recovery." He carefully placed the movie on the counter as he backed out of the room.

Julie watched him go. She turned to Stella. "Give me a second, sweetie. I'll be right back." She rushed out of the room and down the hallway. "Oliver! Wait!" she shouted.

He turned around.

Julie touched his shoulder. "Give her time, okay? Give her time."

Oliver avoided eye contact as he nodded. He broke away from her grasp and continued down the hallway.

He made his way through the sliding doors of the hospital and into the cold rain.

# SUMMER
# AGAIN

# Fix This

The sun danced across the clear blue sky as the birds enjoyed the surprises from the morning dew. It was summer again and almost a year since Oliver first met Stella that night at The Dreslen Piano Bar. Months had passed since the horrible night of the accident and, though Stella was now physically fully recovered, she still had no memory of the accident or her time with Oliver.

Oliver tried many times to reconnect. He hoped that an interaction would spark her memory. One day, he walked into the flower shop and attempted a conversation, but that went nowhere. He even attended one of Julie's barbeques but left early. He tried to start over again, introducing himself, and she was pleasant but distant. When Stella looked at him, there was fear mixed with a hint of sadness in her eyes. And then she would walk away, unable to put her finger on it. Eventually it became too much for him to bear.

It became clear that her memory wasn't going to return, and it became even more clear to him that it was time to leave her alone. It's what was best for her.

Oliver thought he was coping well. He spent less time agonizing over Stella and focused his energy on anything he could be in control of. He vacuumed the rug, he dusted the shelves and sorted every item in his room, he tweaked the pictures again and again until they hung perfectly straight, and once his room was impeccable, he moved on to the rest of the house.

~   ~   ~

Grace sat on the living room couch. She read her magazine in peace until Jack arrived home from work. The second he entered Grace jumped off the couch. "Jack, I'm concerned about Oliver. Look at him."

Jack looked past Grace's shoulder to see Oliver scrubbing the kitchen counters. He then looked around the living room and noticed that everything was perfectly in its place. Their home had never been disorganized, but this was a new level of cleanliness. "This house looks great!"

"Jack!" Grace snapped. "Clearly our son is hurting. Look at him; he's unable to move forward. And now he is taking his emotions out on my kitchen. What do we do?"

Jack took a moment as his demeanor shifted from playful banter to a serious tone. He let out a sigh of frustration as he looked her directly in the eye. "I'm going to fix this," he said. Then he turned back around and rushed out the door.

Grace followed. "Where are you going?" she asked, confused by what just happened and slightly worried about this plan he had instantly concocted in his mind. Jack didn't have the best track record when it came to 'fixing things' in his relationship with Oliver.

"Just give me a couple of hours," he said as he hopped back into his car.

"Jack!"

But it was too late; he had already pulled out of the driveway and headed towards town.

~   ~   ~

The day turned into night and Grace waited in anticipation for Jack to arrive back home. When he finally returned, he walked inside just to tell her that she could go to bed without worry. He told her he would be up late and would fill her in first thing in the morning. This irritated Grace like nothing before; they had always been open with each other. But when he placed his hands on her shoulders and said, "Please, trust me on this one. I'm going to make it better, or at least do my part," she could see in his heart that he was trying so she agreed and made her way to bed.

It was nearly one in the morning and Jack came rushing up the stairs and into Oliver's room. Oliver's lights were on as he still lay there staring at the ceiling, listening to the "Edge of Desire". Jack barged into the room. "Son."

Oliver flinched a little and then slowly tilted his head towards his father.

"Get up. Come on."

Oliver didn't move.

"I get it; you're upset, but it's time to move on."

Oliver rolled his eyes along with his head, back towards the ceiling, completely ignoring his father's words.

"Come on," Jack insisted.

"I don't want to," he said sternly.

Jack grew frustrated and it showed. "We've all had our heart broken, life doesn't always give us what we want or what we ask for."

Oliver knew that. He was living proof of that.

"But you need to stop this pity party."

Something in Oliver snapped. "Just leave me alone!" he yelled.

Jack barked back, "I'm not going to say this again. Suck it up and be a man!"

Oliver lay silent again. He wasn't about to fight. Jack dropped his head in disappointment, with himself this time. He didn't go up there to fight with Oliver or to make him feel worse than he already did. Once he'd calmed down, he said, "I'm sorry. Will you get up and follow me? Please."

Please wasn't something Oliver, or anyone, heard often from his father; however, Jack's stature, tall and tough, and his tone, humble and faint, told two different stories. Warily Oliver slid out of bed and followed him down the stairs.

Jack led Oliver outside. They stood in front of the closed garage. Oliver sighed. "Dad, I don't want to lift with you."

"That's good to hear because that's not what we're doing."

Jack smiled as the garage door rolled its way up to the ceiling exposing the same old garage with a brand-new look. Oliver's jaw dropped as his face began to soften in surprise. There was no longer a grand home gym; in fact, there wasn't one piece of exercise equipment in that garage. Instead it was now filled with a gigantic blank canvas. There were paints of every color of the rainbow and beyond, chalk, ink, and charcoal. Oliver was staring at an artist's heaven.

He looked over at Jack, stunned. He knew that his dad probably didn't know the use of any of the tools he just purchased. And he couldn't imagine him asking a clerk for help to navigate his way through the inventory, let alone stepping foot into a craft store to begin with. Who was the man in front of him?

Jack looked back towards Oliver. "I thought maybe we could use some father-son bonding time."

For the first time ever, Jack's voice felt faint.

"Look, we all know I'm no stranger to the buildup of pain and anger when certain … events don't pan out like we think they should or they don't meet our expectations, but holding on to that anger will start to weigh heavily on your shoulders. It will dampen your mood, blind you to the good things that life surrounds you with, and worse than all that—" he paused and looked Oliver directly in the eye man to man "—worse than that, it will carry over to your other relationships and soon others will pay for someone else's debt. Don't let it destroy your relationships with the ones you love. It will, all of them."

Oliver had never seen this side of his father before. Under that thick-skinned, tough alpha man exterior his father was … sensitive. Like him.

"I don't want you to wake up years down the road to find out that you chose to lose more than the loss you had to endure." Jack cleared his throat. "Besides, I think the both of us could benefit if we let out some of our anger." He smiled softly at Oliver. Jack seemed to lower his guard; he appeared to be vulnerable for once. "What do you say?"

Oliver reached out his arm and placed it on his father's shoulder. He looked back up at his new studio and nodded in approval. "Let's do it."

Oliver and Jack spent the night releasing their frustration, creating art together. They threw paint, got their hands dirty, they screamed and shouted, then sat in mindfulness. They mimicked guitar solos as they danced to the songs of Metallica; they cheered to the words of Bono. They laughed, they told stories, they cried. They began to heal, together.

The night turned into day. With the rise of the sun, Oliver and Jack stood back and admired their painting. The once blank canvas was now filled with every color of emotion. The two men looked back at the cluster of expressions in front of them and they realized they were both more alike than they were different, both equally broken, and now that everything was out in the open they both felt a whole lot lighter.

Jack started to laugh. Oliver followed suit. Seconds later, Jack extended his hand to Oliver, who shook it back with a firm handshake, one his father would approve of. Jack then pulled him in for a loving embrace. Oliver hugged him back.

Grace stood in the door frame in her soft pink morning robe with a cup of coffee in her hand as she watched the prayer she'd been praying for years finally being answered.

STEPHANIE MCBAIN

# FOUR YEARS LATER: AUGUST

# The Drawer

Five years had passed since the accident. Stella had seen pictures of that night in the paper, she talked to the officers at the scene, but as much as she tried to connect, she just couldn't. She had no memory of that night or the events leading up to it. Her last memory before the accident was from August six years ago. She remembered she was getting ready to go to her half birthday, a tradition she loved to partake in. She always said six months living is something to celebrate. That remained true, even more so after the accident.

She remembered that she had bought a new dress and a red flower to go into her hair. She was going to The Dreslen Piano Bar; it was her favorite place to go. A true gem in this town. She was a regular, knew the entire staff and they always took care of her. She remembered she walked into the bar, but that was it. Once she went through the door it was like the film was cut. And then she woke up in the hospital, staring at her best friend, her friend's husband and a strange man who claimed he was her boyfriend, but he wasn't. He couldn't have been. If she was in love, she would have recognized him, right? To her he was a kind guy in town, who brought her a movie, her favorite at that, and who she ran into twice since; once was at the flower shop, where it seemed like he tried to flirt with her but who knew, it was awkward. He was a man of few words. And another time she ran into him briefly at one of Julie's barbeques, but other than saying 'hi' and staring at her funny from across the way, he left abruptly. She never saw him again.

At first Julie would talk to her about him non-stop. She spoke of the two of them so joyfully. She told her how in love they seemed to be and relayed stories that Stella must have told her long ago. Julie was trying to spark a memory within. But these stories didn't make Stella feel better; they actually made her feel worse. She didn't like that she couldn't remember him or that year. She didn't like that she had to relearn parts of her education. She didn't like the feeling of being reminded that there was this chunk of time that was unaccounted for. She tried therapy, she tried past life regression, but nothing seemed to click.

In order for her to move on and not dwell in this 'past,' she had made Julie promise that she would stop talking about this Oliver. She would stop talking about him altogether. This was her wish. And this is what happened.

~  ~  ~

Julie returned home from work one Friday, ready to relax with a much-needed weekend. She grabbed the mail before entering her home. As she walked through the door the peaceful nature drifted away as Geri and Ryan chased each other through the house. Kyle appeared with a two-year-old baby girl in his arms. He gave Julie a kiss. "Welcome home, babe."

"It's good to be back." She looked over at the half-eaten spaghetti on the table. "Are you kids done eating?"

They shouted, "Yes!" as they continued to run around the table.

"Go get ready for bed. Make sure you brush your teeth."

"What about dessert?" Geri yelled.

Kyle barked, "If you didn't finish your meal you don't get dessert."

Julie looked up at Kyle. "That was so hot."

"Was it?"

"Very hot."

"Well, there's more where that came from." He turned toward the kids. "Let's go, kids. Brosse-toi les dents."

The twins ran up the stairs, Kyle followed.

"I love you," Julie called up the stairs.

"I love you too."

Julie sorted through the mail. She paused when she came across a letter addressed to Stella from a Mr. Oliver Roads. She took a deep breath as she walked across the kitchen and opened one of the drawers of the cabinet.

Julie placed the envelope in the drawer just as Stella walked into the room.

"Hey! I thought I heard you come home," she said.

After the accident Stella moved back into her apartment, but a couple months later she and Simon moved into Julie's spare bedroom. It was better for Stella to be around family and, as her protective older sister, Julie wanted her there too.

At the sound of her voice, Julie shut the drawer.

"What's going on?" Stella asked.

"Nothing. You just startled me; that's all."

"What's in the drawer?"

"Nothing."

Stella walked over to Julie and reached for the drawer. Julie placed her body against it refusing to move.

"Julie?"

The two stared at each other for a long moment until finally Julie slowly stepped to the side. Stella cautiously opened the drawer. And inside the drawer and under a pile of old cooking magazines was the stack of letters all addressed to Stella from a Mr. Oliver Roads. She looked back at Julie. "I don't understand. What is this?"

Julie looked back at Stella. "We should talk."

She led Stella into the living room where she told her all about how the letters started to arrive about two years after the accident. Because Stella had told her she didn't want to hear any more about Oliver, Julie didn't show them to her, but she also didn't have the heart to throw them away just in case Stella one day changed her mind or maybe even remembered.

Julie and Stella sat on the couch; the letters, now opened, were spread out across the coffee table.

"Are you mad at me?" Julie asked.

"No," Stella said as she gave her a hug. "You just did what I asked."

The girls shared in a smile. Stella stared back at the letters. "These stories, there is something about them."

Each letter was a story about one of the many adventures Oliver and Stella went on together. Though Stella didn't recall the events she very much enjoyed reading about them. Something about the words created a warm feeling in the pit of her stomach. She also noticed at moments her heart seemed to flutter. *Crazy,* she thought.

Stella reached for one of the letters and, as she picked it up, a postcard, lost in the folded pages, flew out and landed on the floor. Her eyes became wide as she saw the image on the front of the postcard. It was a beautiful charcoal drawing of two shadowed figures sitting on top of a water tower, looking out into the distance as a movie played at the drive-in. She recognized the water tower. It was her spot; the one she always went to every time a picture worth watching was playing on the silver screen.

And even though she didn't remember ever taking someone up there she had been having very vivid dreams lately, dreams of all the activities she loved to do, and there was a presence of a shadowed figure and each time, just as she was about to see his face, she woke up. Her heart began to race.

"Gosh, this explains so much," she whispered.

She looked down at the postcard and noticed that in the bottom right hand corner there was a Los Angeles address and a date for a gallery showing of the artist … Oliver Roads.

# The Gallery

S tella looked up at the tall buildings, the busy city streets, the crowds of people and the hanging lights that seemed to replace the stars. "I'm definitely not in Oklahoma anymore," she whispered to herself.

She wasn't anywhere near Oklahoma, she was in a completely different world called Downtown Los Angeles. At the art walk to be exact. The art walk was an event that took place the last Thursday of each month and it ran throughout the entire summer. It was an event where all the store fronts transformed into works of art. It was a place where many up-and-coming artists were able to display their work in local galleries. That night, Oliver Roads had the pleasure of being one of those artists.

Stella walked up to a glass door that read Featured Artist: Oliver Roads. She peered into the glass walls of the gallery and could see a well-lit room with wood floors and charcoal drawings of every size professionally displayed on each wall. There was a good crowd of people inside the gallery, sipping wine, embracing the messages of the art and enjoying the company they kept with delightful intellectual conversations.

Stella entered the gallery. She stopped at the first portrait. Right in front of her stood a giant canvas. She was struck by its image. She tilted her head in confusion; then, after a moment, she reached her hand out as she gravitated towards the canvas. Suddenly she felt a jolt and retracted her hand as a smile appeared across her face.

At the same time, a handsome man in black slacks and a navy-colored long-sleeved turtleneck, with dark-framed glasses, slightly over grown hair, a wine glass in one hand and an air of mystery witnessed a beautiful girl in her black dress with a long, deep red coat, red lips, a black beret and a new shoulder-length hairstyle, with graceful waves enter the gallery and stop at a giant canvas. He recognized her instantly. He blinked a couple times to make sure his heart and eyes weren't banning together to play tricks on him. When he realized that this woman was real, his heart skipped a beat. He saw her smile and he smiled too remembering how contagious it was and seeing how even years later it could still light up a room. He walked up to her with confidence.

"See something you like?" he asked.

Stella turned to look at the voice. She noticed him right away. The man she had met twice, though more times apparently. The man who had written down all of their stories was now standing next to her. She was stunned for a moment and when she came back to reality she said, "Your drawings, they're beautiful. This one in particular. I like the emotion it's so … real. Like I can feel the joy. If that makes sense."

Oliver chuckled. "It does. And thank you. I had some pretty powerful inspiration."

Stella locked eyes with him. "Me?" she asked.

Oliver's face briefly filled up with a glimpse of hope. Within seconds he managed to contain the emotion once again. His thought was, if he did not get too excited at a possibility, then the disappointment wouldn't be as hard; in fact it just might be bearable. But seeing her here, he just had to ask. He cleared his throat. "Do you remember me?"

There was a pause. Stella still stared into his eyes, putting pieces together in her brain. "No," she said. "But I dream a lot and there is this guy, a shadowed figure, very mysterious. I've never seen his face, but he's in every one of them so I'm thinking he must have been pretty important to me. I'm thinking his name is…" Stella glanced down to the corner of the canvas. She read his name out loud. "Oliver Roads." Then she looked at him once again. In that moment her eyes gave him the green light just as she did years ago.

Oliver smiled. "Come here. I want to show you something."

He grabbed her hand and led her over to the other side of the gallery. They stopped in front of a wall filled with canvases.

Stella took a simple look at the wall and began to cry. Each canvas was another one of Oliver's drawings each with two shadowed figures on an adventure. The figures were watching dueling pianos, watching a drive-in movie from the top of a water tower, singing in a choir at Christmas, bowling, studying, laughing; a cat in meditation, that one made her laugh.

"Wow," she said as she walked closer to the drawings. Each one took her on a whirlwind of emotions. And then her eyes came across one with no shadowed figures. Instead it was two people, clearly drawn. They stood under an umbrella looking into each other's eyes, holding a cup of coffee as the rain poured down.

Stella looked over to Oliver. "This is us."

Oliver nodded. "Yes."

Stella let out a sigh of release as she composed herself. "I feel like I've lived this before. All of it. This is what I dream about."

Oliver walked closer to her. He stood over her shoulder. "Stella, why are you here?" he asked.

She turned his way.

"I'm glad you're here, don't get me wrong; but I sent you many letters, many stories, many invitations. I never heard from you. You never came. Why now?"

"I never saw the others," she said. "Julie thought she was protecting me."

"Protecting you from what?"

"She told me what happened between us. What happened after the accident, how you waited for me; how much you must have loved me. It hurt me not to remember, so I asked her to let us go."

Oliver's eyes began to gloss over. Her words were like warm daggers to his heart.

Stella continued, "I can't remember us. I'm sorry. I don't remember our story. But I know something is missing in my heart. These past couple years I've been on this quest to find out what that is. And the stories you wrote, these drawings, being here in this gallery with you, it feels right."

Emotions poured out of her as she opened up her heart to him once more. "I don't know where you are in life right now and I know we can't change the past, but I was hoping that you and I…"

Stella didn't have a chance to finish her thought because her words slowed down as Oliver came closer to her. He placed his hand on her cheek and they both became lost in each other's eyes.

This was the exact moment he was waiting for, the moment he would have waited a lifetime for—Stella. He leaned in for a kiss and she kissed him back. It was a moment of pure bliss. Suddenly she pulled back.

"Let's grab a cup of coffee. Get to know each other," she said.

They both let out a nervous chuckle.

"I would love that," Oliver said as he blushed.

"Me too."

They smiled at each other and then Stella kissed him again, more passionately this time. Oliver placed his drink on a table as they walked out of the gallery hand in hand.

"Hey, I thought you didn't drink."

"I don't. It was apple juice." They laughed. "Wait, did you just remember?"

"Oh my God, I think I did!"

"Really?"

"No. Julie told me." She laughed. "Would have been neat though."

Oliver joyfully shook his head. "How's Simon?"

"He's handsome."

"Still meditating with you?"

"Every day!"

They laughed as they walked through the crowded city on that perfect night.

"You ready for an adventure?" he asked.

"Of course, Oliver," and with her charm and adorable charisma she added, "Twist." Sealed with a smile and a wink.

### *The End.*

# Create Conversation

Book Discussion Prompts

1.  In the book Oliver and his family moved many times. Have you or anyone you know ever had to move or relocate? How did this effect you/them?

2.  There is a theme of music sending the characters on a journey or a song reflecting their "current mood." Do you relate to music in this way? Do you have a favorite song or lyric that speaks to your soul?

3.  Describe the placement of the vacuum in Oliver's world. What can the placement of this action mean or symbolize?

4.  What character do you most relate to and why?

5.  There are themes of love throughout this book; loving one's self, showing love to another, ideas of what love is supposed to mean or look like. What is your view on love? Is love different than romance? Is there a difference between love and young love?

6.  The characters of the book revisit The Emerald City and The Wonderful Wizard of Oz throughout the story. How does the tale of Dorthey, Toto and her friends reflect Stella and Oliver's life individually and together?

7. The book is broken down into seasons. It could be said that the biggest character growth occurs during fall when Oliver joins the swim team and Stella goes off to college. Would you agree or disagree with this statement? Which moment of the book do you feel changed each their lives the most? Do you have a favorite season?

8. Jack is a character who appears to have a tough exterior, yet we come to find that he is more sensitive than we realized. Describe his relationship with Grace, Oliver and Hannah as well as his position of being a father, son, husband and business man.

9. The author said that Stella and Oliver were "different from each other yet in a unique way similar." Do you agree or disagree? Why?

10. There is a theme of prayer, God, the universe, believing in something bigger than our human self. What are your thoughts on this? As you've experienced life have your beliefs evolved?

11. Discuss and reflect on the evolution of Jack and Oliver's relationship. Can empathy be found in both characters?

12. When Stella and Julie are talking in the flower shop, Stella mentions she had a feeling something was coming. The accident followed shortly after. Have you had an experience in

your own life in which you just knew or moments of intuition?

13. Reflect on Stella's life post-accident. Why do you think she and Oliver didn't connect the same way after the accident like they did before at the Dreslen?

14. This story was originally written as a screenplay. If it were to be made into a movie who would you cast as Oliver and Stella?